The Lunatic

A Novel

By Kevin E. Lake

Copyright Kevin E. Lake 2021

*This work, in part or in its entirety, may NOT be reproduced or distributed, for sale or for free, without the express written permission of the author or the author's representative(s).

*This is a work of fiction. All places, events and characters appearing in this work are products of the author's imagination. Anyone who feels as if they are being represented by any of the characters, events, situations or locations in this work is merely suffering from a guilty conscience.

Prologue

After…

"…911, what's your emergency?"

"She killed him!"

"Who killed who, sir?"

"That Asian whore! She killed him! My neighbor!"

"Who is your neighbor, sir?"

"The agoraphobic day trading pimp that… ah, hell! The lunatic next door!!"

"Sir, are you in danger?"

"Not anymore. I killed her back!"

"You did what?"

"I killed her back! That crazy Asian prostitute! She came over here to kill me next, because she knew that I knew she killed him! The lunatic! He never hurt anyone. He never even left his damn *house*!"

"Sir, we seem to be getting several calls from your vicinity tonight. Is this a Halloween prank? We know where you're calling from, and you can be prosecuted if..."

"This is *not* a fucking joke! She killed that fucking lunatic next door, and then she came over here to kill me!"

(pause)

(heavy breathing)

"Oh, shit!"

"What's wrong, sir? Are you okay?"

"Holy fucking shit!"

"Sir?"

BANG!

"Sir?"

"Sir!"

1

Before...

Well, well, well. Look at that. Will wonders ever cease?

The house next door sold.

I hope whoever bought it has a lot of cash, 'cause they're gonna need it to fix that old heep up. Sure, the bones are good, as the saying goes. It was built more than a century ago. Back when they built houses to last. With real materials. None of this pressboard shit they use on these newer houses. This new crap's not much stronger than cardboard, but the yuppies eat it up, I guess. But no, that house over there will still be standing a hundred years after these newer ones, including mine, have long fallen down.

But the plumbing? The electric? It's gonna all need to be replaced. I'd say whoever the buyers are, they're gonna need to put twenty grand in it, minimum, just to make sure their utilities stay running.

The old bitch that owned it before was nothing more than a slumlord. She owned that house and a few more down the road. Her daddy had money, and she'd inherited everything. Old bitch never worked a day in her life. Never had too. Daddy spoiled her, and that's not uncommon around here.

I live in a very affluent area. Lots of trust babies, like the old man that stays drunk in the woods out here behind my place. Hell, me and my wife- well, my ex-wife, and fuck that bitch, too, by the way- I'll tell you all about *her* later- we were able to get this land we built our house on nearly twenty years ago now because he'd damned near drank up of all his inheritance. He'd be living downtown in the gutter somewhere if it wasn't for the principal of his family's estate being locked up so tight in trust that he can't get his hands on it. He's already sold everything he inherited he *could* get his hands on and liquidate, like these few acres my wife, I mean my exwife- and did I say fuck her?- bought off of him. Stock, property. Hell, all that trust money would be gone if he could get to it, and he'd either be in the gutter downtown, drunk, or, hell, here's a funny thought, he'd be whoring himself out like that prostitute over the other way there. The blonde bimbo that lives on the other side of me. What a skank *that* whore is.

I'm getting ahead of myself here, and I'll come back around to all of it, but let me tell you, the people that live out this way are *nuts*. True *lunatics*! Crazy rich people, that's what I call 'em. Their views of reality are so skewed they have no *idea* what reality is.

But hey, I guess if you're like the old drunk bastard in the woods back there, and your grandparents founded a Fortune Four Hundred company, and no one in your family is going to have to work for generations, why *not* just stay drunk in the woods, right? I think it was Johnson and Johnson, or DuPont Corporation, or something. One of the big blue chips that are too boring for anyone under eighty to own. But hell, when you're born into millions, and I mean literally *millions* of shares of the stuff, how boring would that be? I have no idea what the trust pays out every quarter when the stock pays dividends- hell it might even be Exxon stock- but I'm sure it's in the hundreds of thousands of dollars, if not more than a million. Every damn quarter! Yet somehow, the drunk bastard's always just a buck above broke. It's almost like he's *giving* his money away, he's drinking it up so fast.

And I guess if you're like that whore across the way over there- see, I told you'd I'd come back around to it- and you spread your pretty long legs for all those old rich bastards driving all those BMWs that are always coming and going in out of her driveway and whatnot, then why *not* spend lavishly and get yourself a new BMW yourself every week? I mean, I'm exaggerating a bit, but what I'll say is that that whore gets a new BMW before the one she already has even has a chance to get broken in. Hell, or dirty even, for that matter.

But hell, neither of them are as weird as that sick ass animal hoarder out the other way. The property over on the other side of the one beside me that just sold. Now, we all know about the crazy old cat lady, right? Every town's got one of those.

And every now and then you'll hear some crazy ass story about someone having thousands of chickens or rabbits even. But this guy? He's got everything! Even a freaking camel!

I shit you not!

Dude has a fucking camel running around on his property over there, like a fucking circus animal, and we're just twenty minutes outside of a decent sized city. And if the dude has a fucking camel, what in Science's name other animals might that sick bastard have? Something's not right about that guy and all those animals, and if you ask me, I think there's some beasteality going on over there. I know that sounds like a pretty heavy accusation, but have you seen some of the weird shit on the internet? Someone's making that shit, and I think he might be one of those someones!

And then there's…

….wait…

I see a U-haul pulling up the driveway over there. Let me grab my binoculars and head out here to my storage shed for a better view...

...Yeah, it's a U-haul alright...

… and Science damn if that's not one of those little half electric Priuses pulling in behind it. It's about *time* someone with some sense moved in around here. We are completely destroying this planet. Hell, it's not safe to go outside anymore between the hours of ten o'clock a.m. and four o'clock p.m., because of the size of the hole we've eaten into the ozone layer. Shit, I bet they're lying to us about that, too, *any*way.

Not the hole in the ozone, but its real size and the times of day in which it's really safe to go outside. Hell, I play it safe and *never* go out during the day anymore. These corporations aren't killing *me* off with skin cancer, just so their greedy pharmaceutical arm can milk what little bit of money I have out of me before I die. If the sun's out, I'm not. It's *that* simple.

Hm, he seems to be alone...

...wait a minute, let me adjust my binoculars...

...huh, he looks like some kind of Asian. I can't tell what kind. At least from here. And no, that's not racist, me saying 'some kind of Asian.' He *is* some kind of Asian, so it is what it is and that's all that it is, and I can assure you that I am the *least* racist person you will *ever* meet in your life. I am a progressive liberal who votes Democrat.

Well, I *used* to vote Democrat, back when I used to vote, but I am so detached from politics now, the dog and pony show that it is…

...look, when it comes to politics, the left and the right are two wings of the same bird. Sadly, it took me years to figure that out. They had me fooled as much as anyone, thinking my vote actually counted and all. If that were true, there'd be no Electoral College.

But listen, when it comes to social issues, there's right- wait, terrible word to use here- there's correct, and there's incorrect. Progressive liberalism is correct. And that right winged conservative crap? Look, there is no room for hate in this world. Period. The mass death and destruction that has come from hate throughout history speaks for itself, and this is exactly why I got out of following politics and voting years ago. How can that man in the White House, a Democrat, at least for now, preach to me about 'reaching across the aisle' and 'getting along with the opposition' and all that hippity blah blah blooh blah, when that man across the aisle (*rarely* a woman, because the Republicans are misogynists) is a white supremicist? I will *not* be reaching across the aisle to a conservative, misogynistic white supremicist! I will harbor nothing but hatred in my heart for him, and any and all who voted to put him in power, and if I was the man in the White House, I would round them all up and send them to the fucking showers, and yes, you know *exactly* the kind of showers I'm talking about!

...you know, come to think of it, the woman that lived over there last was Asian. She was adorable, but her husband was a prick.

Now *there's* another Science damn story for you. Talk about *lunatics*, like the rich drunk bastard back here in the woods, and the high dollar whore across the way, and that eccentric animal hoarder who *has* to be rich as hell in order to be buying up all those exotic animals like camels and shit, well that bastard married to that young Asian woman that used to live over there in the house that just sold was a rich prick, too. And a lunatic? Pure definition of the word!

He wasn't born into it, his money that is, like the drunk bastard back in the woods behind me and probably the animal hoarder. He earned his, like the whore across the way. He wasn't a gigolo, but he may as well have been. He was one of these YouTuber guys. Whored his life out to strangers on the internet and made a fucking killing doing it. Hell, when he and that pretty little mail order bride of his first moved in over there- and no, I can't remember what kind of Asian she was, and remember, that's not racist to say that, because I'm a progressive liberal, so there's no *way* I can be racist, for the life of me, I just can't remember what kind of Asian she was- I think Thai, maybe- they could hardly afford to pay the twelve hundred dollars a month rent. Three years later, which has been about as many years since they left, leaving the house empty that whole time until now, he was able to buy a fifty acre farm on the other end of the county! Right up against the James River so the son of a bitch can go catfishing from his backyard any time he wants!

And the way he did it? Specifically? Well, we'll get into that later, too. Maybe after I tell you all about that blonde whore across the way. Hell, she even tried to sell *me* some lovin' one time, but I simply told her I couldn't afford it when I saw her coming. No, I never heard anything about price, because I didn't want her to lure me into trying to Jew her down, which I might have tried, because, yeah, she's a whore, but she's pretty easy on the eyes if you know what I mean.

And no, that was not anti-semetic for me to say that. Jew her down. Everyone knows exactly what that means. It's just an expression, and we've already made it quite clear that I am a progressive liberal, so I absolutely, positively can*not* be anti-semtic. My heart goes out to all those poor bastards who were sent off to those camps, though I'll tell you, I think that's exactly what we should do with all these fuckers who supported that *last* guy in the White House. That real estate investing fabulous showman that he was. Hell, at least the little weakling in there now gives mouth movement about reaching across the aisle to get along with the opposition, even though I will *never* get along with white supremacists, homophobes, xenophobes. You name it! They're all of it! But that last guy? Whew, well, you know all about *him*. Four years of hating every*one* and every*thing* that wasn't part of the white straight male establishment.

But hey, for now I've gotta keep my eyes on this Asian dude moving in next door. I wonder if he's related to that lady that used to live over there? Or if maybe they at least know each other? I heard they're clannish and stick together and all that, those Asians. Boy, did I feel sorry for her for being married to that arrogant prick Nazi bastard she was married to. That arrogant *rich* prick Nazi bastard, now. Another crazy fucking rich person. Pure lunatic. There are few types of people in this world that I hate more than conservatives, and that's crazy rich people. Nothing but a bunch of fucking luntatics!

2

So it's been about a week, and I swear to Science, other than the day I saw that Asian guy move in next door, I haven't seen him since. I mean, he has *not* come *out* of that house since moving in!

Now, I could have sworn he was alone that day he moved in. I mean, there were a couple of guys helping him unload the U-Haul, and they both looked a little light in the slippers if you know what I mean, but they left, eventually, and I watched him, from this super secret squirrel place out by one of my outbuildings where I can pretty much see everything going on over there- and that's all another story in and of itself- and I saw him wave his helpers off. Turns out that little Prius wasn't his, afterall, because those two guys that helped him move in- you know, the ones that seemed a little light in the slippers- got in it, and they drove off after they'd unloaded the U-Haul. Now, he *did* leave in the U-haul to take it back, I guess, and he came back in a little BMW, that unless I've been missing something, I haven't seen leave his driveway since.

And no, I'm not homophobic because I said those guys that helped him move in were light in the slippers! It's just an expression, and I only used it so you'd know they were gay without me having to come out and say they were gay, because it's no one's business but theirs!

Listen, if a man wants to be a queer, then he has every right to be a queer. That's his business. I've already made it clear where I stand, but alas, I must state my case again, simply because I know there'll be someone out there trying to twist my words, because I said those guys were light in the slippers. I guarandamntee you I am the *least* homophobic person you will ever meet in your life. I'd vote for a queer to be president, as long as he, or she mind you, was a Democrat. And, well, if I still wasted my time voting. What a dog and pony show that business is.

So anyway, after those two queers left, the Asian dude went in his house, and I swear to *Science* it's like he vanished. I mean, you'd think he'd have to at least come out to go to work. But hell, I already told you most of the lunatics around here are rich, so maybe he is, too. Maybe he's got so much money he doesn't *have* to work.

And in case you're wondering, I don't hate rich people because I'm envious of what they have that I don't. I hate them because they're greedy and they're arrogant. Even the ones that don't go around showboating and bragging. They're trying to come off as humble, but you can tell they're looking down their noses at you while they stand there, not saying much if you ever find yourself talking to one of them for some reason. They're just trying to come across as if they are all normal and stuff, acting like they're just like the rest of us and all that. Well, that's *all* it is, an *act*, and I can see right through it. I'm not stupid. Actually, I'm probably the smartest person you'll ever meet.

Besides, I could have been rich if I'd wanted to be. *Anyone* could be rich. All you have to do is be greedy and go out and make a lot of money. I mean, I wasn't born into it like the drunk out back in the woods, and hell, probably that animal hoarder. I'm sure he was born into it. A fucking camel of all things?

Jeesh!

But the whore across the way and that asshole that used to live over there where that Asian guy just moved in last week- that Nazi prick with his mail order bride- they *all* made their own money. And I'm *way* smarter than all of those dumbasses put together.

I was well on my way to making a lot of my own money until my first wife cleaned me out. She was just pissed because I always told her that once I made a certain amount each year I was going to donate the rest- what we didn't need to live off of- to charities. Like Bill and Melinda Gates. Now *there* are a couple of social justice warriors who are doing it *right*!

...wait a minute. Terrible word to use...

...who are doing it *correctly*!

Where do I work?

I don't work anywhere. I'm not a sheep!

I work for myself. Here from home.

What kind of work do I do?

I'm a machinist by trade, but what I actually do is build boats.

Yes, boats!

The damned good, solid and expensive kind, that's what kind!

I build custom built, handmade yachts. And I make them mostly out of wood, in the classic tradition.

Did you know that most of these crazy rich people around here have yachts? Yes, even though we're four hours away from the ocean and there's only one lake between here and there, Lake Anna, big enough for a yacht, but I don't think you understand just how rich some of these fuckers around here are. And I *know* they have yachts. They pay out the nose to buy them, and they pay out the nose again to keep them moored up down there at the beach. Hell, a lot of these rich bastards have a yacht down there at the beach, or the Chesapeake Bay, and even down across the state line at the Outer Banks. I mean, these lunatics are freaking *rich*! Could you imagine? Three freaking yachts for one person?

And do you know what the markup on those boats are? I mean, do you know what the markup on almost everything is? It's *outrageous*, and it ought to be *illegal*!

All these companies making this and making that. And they don't give a shit about the products or the people they sell them to. All they care about is profit! And no, don't call me a communist or a socialist, because I believe in one's right to make money, but there really needs to be a cap. Hey, they have salary caps in professional sports, so there should be profit caps in business. Personally, I take social responsibility and cap my own profits.

Okay, so here's how I do it. It costs me about one hundred thousand dollars in materials, time and labor to build one of my wooden yachts. Yeah, that's a lot of money, time and effort, but I'm telling you, they are the best custom, handmade yachts you can buy. I was really, really good in shop class back in high school. So I know what I'm doing.

So, the average U.S. annual income is around forty five thousand dollars a year. I sell my boats for one hundred and forty five thousand dollars each, because it takes me about a year to make one. The reason it takes so long is because it's very detailed work. And in the end, and at that selling price, it allows me to be average, which is good enough for me, and which should be good enough for everybody.

Hey, I don't need to be like these arrogant rich lunatics around here who look down their noses at everybody who isn't as rich as them. Equal with others is okay with me, and anyone who wants anything more than equal is greedy and arrogant. *Exactly* why I hate rich people.

So anyway, my first wife, she was all on board with the boat business. And she didn't mind so much that my profit margin was what it was. She felt comfortable with it, because she had a sales job. She sold health insurance. So she earned commissions, and hell, she had some pretty big months, too, because you know, you *have* to have health insurance. You're a fucking idiot if you don't have health insurance, not to mention a fucking burden on the rest of society who is responsible enough to carry it. And if you *don't* have health insurance, *you* are going to be the one to get that dreaded brain eating amoeba and no one will treat you for it, because you don't have insurance. And no, I'm not being facetious. It's true. That's just how Murphy's law works. So only a self-centered idiot wouldn't carry health insurance.

Anyway, there were a few months there where I needed a little help. I'd run out of funds to get past the main hull of the boat I happened to be working on at the time, and she floated me some money. I mean, why shouldn't she have? She was my wife. We were married. Partners. Not to mention the fact, from a pure monetary standpoint that she had it and I didn't so she should have just given it to me anyway.

Long story short, after she'd floated me some funds for a few months, she told me she wasn't floating me any more. She said I had to either figure out how to find the funds elsewhere to finish the yacht I happened to be working on at that time or get a job.

Are you fucking serious? I have a few bad months where I'm stuck on the particular boat I was working on at the time and she's acting like she's the boss of me?

Anyway, I ended up going to the bank to get a business loan to get me past the point where I was. I walked in, knowing I'd get approved, because I *am* a white male and all that. And no, I'm not being snooty about it. What I'm saying is, I'm very aware of my privilege. I do my best not to take advantage of it, and I feel guilty as hell about it, because I knew this one colored kid back in shop class that was really good with woodwork, too, and I guarandamntee you they'd never give *him* a loan if he needed one, I'm sure, because he was colored, and the banking system is as racist as those Science damned Republicans. I mean, who do you think owns the banks? It's sure not a bunch of inner-city blacks just trying to make ends meet. It's the Grand Old Party that owns the banks, that's who!

Anyway, sure enough, they were going to approve me for enough money to get past the point where I was stuck, but they said I needed a co-signer. Would you believe that bitch refused to co-sign? Gave me some lecture about how I never finished anything I started, and how she wasn't going to risk her credit score on a bad load for *me*. Told me she was tired of being the only one to make any money, and, well, we ended up arguing. I may have pushed her, but it was only because I felt threatened. She was really yelling at me, and I didn't feel safe. I was simply trying to add distance between us so I would feel safe in my space. She was *totally* inside my bubble! It's not that I was pushing her as much as it was that I was creating my safe space.

Long story short, that bitch ended up going off and filing for divorce. We didn't have any kids. I've never fathered children, though I did have a couple of step kids with my second wife. I, personally, would *never* bring a child into this Science-forsaken world. Anyone who would is a stupid idiot.

So anyway, since there were no kids involved, the divorce was a quickie. We were renting a house at the time, and I was building the yacht I was working on at the time in a rental garage a few milies away, so I said fuck it, and I just moved into the garage I was renting. But that didn't last long, because I soon figured out the solution to my money problems and my living arrangements. Believe it or not, the answer came from the same place I'd honed my boat building skills. My old high school shop class.

...wait a minute...

...wow, that blonde bimbo whore from across the way just pulled up to that Asian guy's house over there in her BMW. It's hard for me to see, because there's only one spot I can really get a clear view, because of all the trees that asshole who lived over there a few years back planted, but I can...

...let me get my binoculars...

...shit! She's not alone!

Holy hell! There's *another* whore with her...

...hold on, let me adjust my focus...

...wow! That other fucking whore is smoking hot!

And she's *Asian!*

I can't tell what kind of Asian, though. Some kind of Asian! And son of a *bitch* does she look cute as a button in the tight little mini-skirt she's wearing!

Damn, so the little blonde tramp from across the way is making a housecall on this new guy over there, and she's bringing a partner!

Yup, I guess that settles it. Whoever this new guy is over there, this some kind of Asian guy, he's fucking loaded, just like the rest of these lunatics around here! He doesn't have to work, because he's already got so much money, and one whore isn't good enough for him, so he calls out for *two* whores. And it looks like he's at least *partly* into his own kind. I *told* you I heard those Asians were clannish like that.

Science damn!

Like Rod Stewart used to say, some guys have all the luck!

3

No further evidence needed! That Asian guy next store is a total fucking lunatic! Not only is he obviously rich- I mean, two whores at a time?- he's obviously a sex feind, too. I mean, two whores at a time? Do I need to say it again?

I'll tell you though, for the past month or so, since the first time I saw the blonde whore from across the way roll up in there with that Asian whore friend of hers, I've been a bit intrigued. That Asian girl going back and forth to that new guy's house is one *hell* of a looker. I mean, I've not gotten up close to her or anything, but she sure as hell looks good from a distance through my binoculars.

And yes, I know for a *fact* they're whores. Like I said, the blonde one tried to sell me her, well, you know what she tried to sell me. The beauty that lies between her thighs, *that's* what.

Oh, it was probably six years ago or so now when she solicited me. I'd actually gone over to that house next door, where the Asian guy who never comes out lives now, when that last couple moved in. I was actually trying to do the neighborly thing. Gee, let me tell you. No good deed goes unpunished. I mean, they were rude as shit to me, and all I was trying to do was introduce myself to them, and hell, help them understand the danger they were in.

Now, the day I met them, they'd told me exactly where they were from, but for the life of me I can't remember. Probably because I didn't really care. Just being honest. I know he talked funny and said he was from Kentucky or West Virginia. Hell, I don't know. Maybe it was Arkansas. One of those hillbilly states. The girl, and let me tell you, she was *gorgeous*, was from one of those third world shitholes in Southeast Asia. I think it was Cambodia or Thailand or something like that.

And no, that's not culturally insensitive of me to refer to those places as shitholes, because they are. The last guy in office got blasted for saying that about those places, but that was all a setup on his part. He wanted people to jump in and take up for the reputations of places like those third world shitholes to distract them from the fact that those places are still third world shitholes because of U.S. corporations taking advantage of them. It was a smoke and mirrors play on his part to distract everyone. So, while they're rushing to defend the reputations of those places, like Puerto Rico, or wherever it was he'd said it about, he was just grinning ear to ear, knowing his CEO buddies who'd gotten him into office were still over in those shitholes raping their resources for profit and their women and children for fun. I know all of this to be true, because even though I don't vote in the dog and pony show anymore, I am still, and will remain until my dying day, an informed progressive. Hey, I read journals and watch the news. You remember what Mark Twain said about the news. People who don't follow the news are uninformed. Well, I follow the news, so I am *not* uninformed, let me tell you!

Anyway, when the girl told me where she was from- hell, it might have even been Maylasia- all I did was ask them if they were scared about the fact that the man up in the White House was trying to deport her. That's all I asked, and *man*, did they become real *assholes!*

The guy starts telling me about how his wife was here legally, and about how they'd spent more than a year going through the immigration process, and they'd paid a lawyer, like, five thousand dollars to help them, and that the guy up in the White House was only trying to deport immigrants who were here illegally.

"Sounds like you like him," is all I said. Then the guy tells me about how he doesn't give a shit about politics. I didn't believe him. If he didn't give a shit about politics then he would have hated that guy up in the White House as much as me and anyone else who had a heart for others hated him. I mean, Science damn, the son of a bitch was trying to deport this guy's wife, whether he wanted to accept that fact or not! Oh, but don't try confusing a conservative with facts. They *hate* that shit!

"I like him," the girl said. Can you believe that? Here that guy up in D.C.- and let me tell you, you talk about a lunatic, that guy was a fucking lunatic- but here he was, trying to kick her out of the country, and she claimed to actually like him?

"How in the hell could you like a guy who's trying to deport you?" I asked her.

"He no try to deport me," she said in broken English. You could tell she was obviously an uneducated peasant girl from some village out in the jungle somewhere. But I have to admit, her accent was cute. And boy was she pretty. I think she was in her thirties, even though her husband was almost fifty, but she looked nineteen, if that. Real petite and pretty, and everyone knows Asian women age better than white women. She was definitely one of those mail order brides, and I always wondered how much he paid for her.

"He only deport lawbreaker," she said. "He has balls. Man with no balls no man."

Wow! So I guess her husband had brainwashed her with his political views. So, I knew already that this guy over here beside me, the one who rented over there for three years before getting filthy rich the dumbest way I've ever seen- and I'll be telling you all about *that* later- was one of those Science damn Nazi types that needed to be sent off to the showers, and you know what showers I'm talking about. The kind people like him came up with!

Oh sure, he was married to an Asian girl, but that was just to disguise the truth. The truth is that he hated minorities and immigrants, and he just wanted to throw everyone off, so he went and married one. I mean, that has to be it, right? Otherwise he would have hated the president at the time, just like me and everyone else that has a heart for others. That's okay, because he couldn't fool me. I knew right then and there that I was living beside a white supremisist Nazi. I'm not stupid. I'm probably the smartest guy you'll ever meet.

Anyway, that's when it happened. That's when that little blonde whore from across the way tried to sell me the beauty that lies between her thighs.

I'd had enough of talking to that Nazi and his little brainwashed mail order bride for that day, even though the conversation had just gotten started, so I went back out to the end of the driveway to the road to walk up to my driveway, and the blonde whore who lives across the way pulled into *her* driveway, right at the same time.

So, that blonde whore stopped and got out of her car to open her gate. She has a long driveway that goes up to her house, and the bitch makes so much money selling herself that she even has a couple of horses. Just like so many of the other rich lunatics around here. So she has to have a gate to keep them in. Something I wish that crazy rich bastard with the camel and all the other exotic animals would do. Get a gate to keep that camel in. Oh, I'll get to that later.

Anyway, I noticed she was driving yet *another* new BMW. I was just admiring the color- a hue of blue like I'd never seen, and I was thinking that it would make a nice color for my next yacht, once I sold the one I was working on at the time, of course- and she gets out of the car, all decked out in a skirt so short it barely covered her panties, and she looks over at me and she says, "like what you see?" And she smiled real big, and let me tell you, I was tempted, but I just said, "I can't afford it." She smiled even bigger and said, "Oh, come on now, hon. I bet we can squeeze something into your budget."

Talking dirty like that was getting to me, so I knew I had to get out of there. I just said, "sorry. I'm not rich like everyone else around here. I work for what I've got. I gotta go."

I turned and started walking up the road to my driveway, and she called out behind me, "I'm a hard working woman myself. I can prove it to you if you give me the time. I'm even willing to lower my price for such a nice guy like you."

I almost started running to get away from that dirty whore, because dirty whore though she is, she's nice to look at, and I was actually thinking about taking out a cash advance on one of my credit cards and buying me some of that beauty that lies between her thighs. I didn't do it, and if I see her outside now, I make sure to go the other way entirely to avoid any temptation.

So my day started out really shitty.

Literally!

I stepped in a big heaping pile of camel shit, and then to top it off, when I slid and almost fell, I almost fell into the ass end of the Science damned camel that had shit in my yard in the first place. Well, I guess this rushed up the story about the camel and that son of a bitch that owns it needing a gate! I mean, I've seen that freaking camel in other people's yards, but this is the first time it's ever come into mine.

So, what I was doing was making my way back to the only part of my property where I can still look over and see the lunatic's house next door. Yeah, the Asian guy that moved in. I've given up on seeing him. Hell, maybe he's a damned vampire. I mean, he's been over there for more than a month now, and other than the day he moved in, I *still* haven't seen him.

But that's okay, because it's that little Asian whore that keeps coming around that I'm trying to see. I guess he prefers her over the blonde whore across the way there, because the blonde whore only comes over about half the time that the little Asian whore comes over. She comes over quite a bit. And hell, he must be paying her a pretty penny, because I've already seen her pulling up in two different brand new BMWs since he's moved in and she's started coming around, and again, that's only been a month. Can you imagine how rich these fucking lunatics living all around me are? When you can afford to pay your whores enough for them to pretty much become rich, too, and go buy a new BMW any time they want?

Well, anyway, I used to be able to see pretty much my neighbor's entire property over there, where the lunatic Asian guy lives now, but that last bastard that lived over there planted a bunch of Science damned evergreen trees on the property line to block my view. Sure, he probably saw me pulling back from the window a time or two and thought maybe I was trying to see what him and that cute little Asian woman I'm sure he bought and paid for were doing, but I wasn't. I was just admiring the view. I mean, even though they were just renting, they took really good care of the place, and it looked really nice. I'll admit, my place kind of looks like shit. All grown up with weeds. Fallen trees and limbs everywhere. But look. Mowing grass or trimming weeds is the same as making your bed. Just as you're going to mess your bed up the night of the day you've made it, causing you to just have to make it again the next day, you're just going to have to go back out there and mow the grass or trim the weeds a week later, because the grass and weeds are going to just keep growing. You can pick up all the sticks and limbs that you want, but more are just going to fall.

Anyway, I didn't mind him doing it so much at first, putting up all those trees, because I still had plenty of places I could watch them from outside, one place in particular where I had a pretty wide view. Again, I was only watching to see what kind of flowers that cute little mail order bride of his was planting and whatnot, but then one day he had a damn commercial sized truck come in with some commercial sized leyland cypress trees on it to block the last of what view I had of the place- I mean, these things were fifteen feet tall- and *that's* where I drew the line!

What did I do?

I called his fucking landlady!

Like I said earlier, she was pretty much a slumlord, and I never cared for her- just another rich lunatic who inherited her wealth if you ask me- but she had a right to know what was going on on her property. Renters aren't allowed to make changes like that. Not without permission.

Long story short, she said she *knew.* She said he'd called and asked permission, and she said she told him to go ahead and do it. She even said she asked him to plant a tree for her! I asked her if she paid for it, and she said of course not. Said the guy wouldn't let her, and that he'd be honored to plant a tree for her. What a fucking lunatic!

I'll tell you, I was *pissed!* That arrogant bastard was paying three grand for those cypress trees just to not have to see my house and my, like I've said, not so well manicured lot! And to block my view of his place! What an arrogant prick! And I know the cost of those trees, because I saw the name of the nursery on the side of the truck, and I called down there the next day and asked for a quote. That's how I knew it was three grand!

There's no way that son of a bitch thought he was so important that I was spending all my time watching him, did he? I mean, if I wanted to know what he was doing all I had to do was wait for him to upload his daily YouTube videos. And yes, I always watched those. And the only reason he got rich from that shit is because people are stupid and because of that fucking camel that came over here and shit in my yard today. The camel whose ass my head almost went up when I slid in its shit. A two humped camel named Sally, I came to find out from that eccentric queer bastard that owns her. Science knows how many other exotic animals he's hoarding over there. I guess I'll find out when they make their way over here to my place like that Science damned camel did.

And no, I'm not homophobic for saying queer bastard. We've gone over this. I don't hate the guy and call him a queer bastard because he's gay. That's *his* business. I hate him and call him a queer bastard because he's just another crazy rich lunatic who doesn't keep his animals on his property. He's got no respect for those of us who he obviously considers to be beneath him.

Anyway, for the three years that house next door sat empty, I did a lot of thinking. I am always doing a lot of thinking. It's one of the things that makes me such a good yacht builder. It's why I was so good in shop class in high school. I think about a thing a million times before I do it. Sure, it takes it longer to get the thing done, but when it *does* get done, it gets done correctly. Do it right, do it once, that's my motto. I make the mistakes in my mind, so I don't make them in practice.

So anyway, while that house next door was empty, I did two things, fearing that that old slumlord would die, her kids would get the house and then they'd sell it, and as it turns out, that's obviously exactly what happened. I guess she died. She was close to ninety the last time I talked to her. That was the time I called her about that arrogant misogynist Nazi over there with the mail order bride planting those trees. After that, when I'd call, no one answered the phone. So obviously she's dead. And obviously her kids who were just waiting around on her to die so they could inherit her money sold the house. And that crazy rich Asian bastard- the one who is so rich he can afford two whores at a time- bought it. But the point I was trying to make was, what if the house was sold to another white supremicist type? I needed to know what was going on over there at all times, so I needed a surveillance system.

The first thing I did was install security cameras all over my property. I put them on the outside of the house and on the inside. I put one in the living room aiming right at the front door so I can see if anyone breaks in while I'm down in the basement working on my yachts. And I've got one in the back of the house, at the same angle, watching the back door. I've got so many of them outside that if anyone steps on my property from any direction I'll know while I'm down in the basement working on my yachts.

Okay, so number two? And, well, I don't know if I should admit this or not, but I will. I took out one of those cypress trees.

I wasn't going to make it obvious by just cutting down a tree, but what I did was I picked a spot on the side of the property where no one who's ever lived over there ever went much, right where the Nazi had planted those cypress trees, and then I took a hatchet one night and I cut into one of those leyland cypress trees just a little past halfway on the westward facing side. You see, for some reason, in the months of November and March, we get these really heavy winds coming from the west. It took two years, but with a combination of the westerly winds and insect damage where I'd hacked the tree, it fell into the one beside it, giving me the perfect view of the front and the back of the house next door from a side angle.

Well, anyway, I was heading over there this morning to see if I could get a glimpse of that Asian hooker coming out and leaving. I'd seen her BMW pull in just at dark last night, and I knew she'd spent the night, because, well, okay, I set some cameras up over there, too, and the one that is set up to watch the driveway never got triggered. I set them up at some point during the three year period that the house was empty.

Hey, it was for my own protection. Like I said, what if another Nazi moved in over there?

I actually went out and did something else I never thought I'd *ever* do while that house over there sat empty. I went out and bought a little pistol. A .38 special. I hate guns, and I think they should be illegal, but until they are, I'm going to have one, because I need one to protect me from all of the lunatics out there that have them.

Anyway, back to that little Asian whore. I'll admit it. She might be a whore, and she might be out of my price range, like her buddy the blonde whore across the way, but man is she smoking hot. What I wouldn't give to take a peek up one of those short little ass hugging skirts she's always wearing when she's coming and going. Must I quote Rod Stewart again? I mean, how do all these nutcases, like the guy next door, and that arrogant Nazi that lived there before him, get all these hot bitches, when guys like me get, well. I mean, I'm not trying to be mean. And yes, fuck my exwife. That bitch. All she did was use me. But, well. What I'm trying to say is that she was not very easy on the eyes.

Okay, she was fucking ugly!

You remember Bride of Frankenstein? Well, she didn't look like her. She looked like Frankenstein!

Yeah, yeah, yeah. I'm going to get to her. How we got together. Why she left.

Anyway, I'm sneaking around over there, not really paying attention to my footing, and I step in the biggest pile of animal shit I've ever seen in my *life*. I started to fall forward and I caught myself just before my head went up that camel's ass. It was standing there eating the leaves off of a fucking tree staring at me like *I* was the one trespassing.

"What the fuck!" I shouted.

"Sorry," I heard someone say. I look over, and here comes that eccentric animal hoarding queer. I mean, let me tell you. The guy *has* to be gay. There is *no way* he is not gay. He's about fifty years old and good looking as hell. I mean, he looks like a movie star. And he's single? Okay, good looking plus single equals gay in *my* book. But that's okay with me, being a progressive liberal and all, but his Science damned camel in my yard?

Not okay!

"I don't know how she got out, but I am so sorry. I'll take her back," he says.

"You're Science damn *right* you'll take her back!" I told him. "Why the *fuck* do you have a camel, anyway?"

"Well, Sally came to me by way of…"

"Sally?" I said. "Like the kid song? Sally the camel has two humps and all that shit?"

"Yeah," the guy said, and he smiled like that would make me like him or something. These fucking crazy rich people think we're all stupid. Well, I'm *not* stupid, and all his smile did was piss me off even more.

"Get your Science damn camel Sally and her two fucking humps off my property, and if I ever see her over here again I'm going to fucking shoot her and eat her!"

That was a bluff, of course, because I only have that little .38 and I don't think it would do the trick on an animal of that size, and I'm sure as shit not going to make an animal suffer. I just got the .38, like I said, for self defense, because let me tell you, something I hate as much as rich people and conservatives is guns. They're just not safe. They need to be outlawed, but until they are, you'd better believe I'm keeping one to protect myself from all of the gun nuts out there that have them.

Guns are one of the biggest problems this fucking country has. There wouldn't be all these damn school shootings and massacres if it wasn't for all these guns. Speaking of massacres, you remember that one out in Vegas a few years back? The worst, so far, in American history? That was carried out by an older white guy married to some mail order bride from Southeast Asia, and let me tell you, that white Nazi and his little mail order bride, the YouTubers, were actually living over there next door to me when that massacre in Vegas happened. I slept with one eye open the rest of the time they lived over there after that. I mean, that guy could have been the next one to carry something like that out, and with me living right next door to him, who do you think his first target would be? As much as I hated to do it, I went out and got that little .38 special to keep me safe from the next lunatic who might move in next door.

I bought the gun off a guy who knew a guy, you know. Not that I'm against registering firearms or anything, I just think the Government doesn't need to know *every* Science damn thing we have going on. I mean, I know I'm a post middle aged white male, which fits part of the standard profile of a domestic terrorist, but like I've been telling you, I'm a progressive liberal who used to vote Democrat when I was still naive enough to vote, so *my* guns shouldn't have to be registered. I'm the last person in this country that would ever shoot anyone, unless, of course, it was in self defense. But these fucking Nazis? The hell with registering their guns. They shouldn't even be allowed to *have* them!

Anway, the asshole with the camel actually started fucking crying on me. He wasn't boo-hooing and bawling or anyway, but tears were running down his face as he took Sally the two humped camel by the reins and started walking her off my property.

Remember what I told you about suspecting that crazy rich bastard of committing beasteality? I mean, have you seen some of the shit that's on the internet? Well, someone's making that shit, and I wouldn't be surprised at all if he's not one of those someones. I mean, the way he freaking cried when I insulted his camel just proves that that animal is more than just a pet, and I guarandamntee you it's his damn lover!

Anway, to make matters worse, just as he starts heading off with that camel, I heard a car door slam. I turned around, and there goes that Asian whore's BMW down the lunatic next door's driveway. *Science damn it!* That camel and that eccentric animal fucking queer that owns her made me miss seeing what I'd come out here to see! Damn, I'm telling you, she looks good in those tight little skirts, and I'd love to get just one peek up one of them some day.

But I guess today was not the day.

Maybe tomorrow.

5

Stepping in camel shit is one thing, but stepping in rich guy?

Yeah, I'm serious!

It hasn't happened in a while, but back when my wife and I, well, back when my ex-wife and I bought this place, it used to happen all the time.

You see, the crazy rich bastard that stays drunk in the woods out back sold us the property. At one point or another he owned most of the land around here, him and that slumlord that used to own the house next door before she died and that crazy Asian lunatic bought it from her kids. Hell, they might have been related, that old slumlord lady and the drunk out back. Probably brother and sister. I don't know.

By the way, I *still* haven't seen him since he moved in, that crazy Asian lunatic. He's a total agoraphobe. Afraid to leave the house. I've been like that before, and it sucks. But hey, at least he's got all that money to be able to afford to pay for those two whores to come and please him whenever he wants. I thought for a while there he was going to just settle for the one- the Asian whore- but that little blonde bimbo from across the way still goes over there every now and then, so I guess he still has his moments when he wants to do the old threesome thing. And that little Asian whore of his goes over to the blonde bimbo's house quite a bit. I'm kind of thinking they might be roommates. Well, at least when the Asian whore is not staying at the Asian lunatic's house next door. Whatever. I know when *my* agoraphobia kicks in it sure would be nice to be able to call for an order of Asian whore with a side of blonde bimbo to go with my pizza delivery. Must be nice being rich.

Anyway, I guess the crazy rich drunk bastard out behind me here used to get blackout drunk and wander around in the woods thinking he still owned them all, and he'd just pass out drunk wherever he happened to be when he'd had enough booze to pass out. I was out there one morning, I think during our first month of living here, just after they'd finally finished building the house and all the storage sheds I had them build so I could store all of my yacht building equipment and supplies, and I freaking *tripped* over the guy.

I hadn't really been paying attention to where I was going, because the people who were renting next door at the time- and mind you, this is going *way* back to before that misogynistic Nazi guy and his little Asian mail order bride ever lived over there- where over there doing something in the yard. I think they were setting up one of those slip and slide things for their kids- they had kids, and Science damn were they loud- I hate kids and do *not* understand why *anyone* would bring any more of them into this fucked up world- but anyway, they were setting up a slip and slide I think, and I wanted to watch. I've always been fascinated by how people can take joy in children. It makes no sense to me. It's definitely a liking of the lower minded. People born of a lesser metal than me.

Anyway, I tripped over this crazy rich drunk bastard. It woke him up, and I walked him back up to his house. He was still drunk from the night before- had to be- and he was going on and on about how his father never loved him. I don't know, maybe his rich old man sent him off to boarding schools just to get rid of him when he was a kid like most rich bastards, or something like that. Anyway, he was always bitching about how he'd never received an ounce of love from his father, but that was okay, because by Science he was making sure to give it to others, or something like that. Never heard him bitch and complain one time, though, about how his father left him a Science damned fortune!

Hey, my dad never sent me off to boarding school, because we weren't rich, but it's not like he was there much. He worked all the time and acted like he was paying attention to me when he was around, even though I knew he wasn't. But you don't hear *me* bitching and moaning about it. Besides, that crazy old rich drunk bastard is well into his seventies now. You've gotta get over that shit sometime, right?

After a while I guess it kind of kicked in that he didn't own this place over here anymore and he stopped passing out drunk over here all the time. He used to do it monthly. Now he does it about once a year, usually in the summer I guess because the weather's nice enough for him to wander this far away from his house. I still help him get home, and he's still always bitching and moaning about his dad. All these years later. Daddy never loved me, wah, wah, wah. That's okay, because I give it to others, wah, wah, wah. His dad's probably been dead for half a damn century already. Jeesh!

I actually tried to help the guy once. Beyond just walking him home while he was still drunk from the night before- he *had* to be. Passed out in my woods like he was. Anyway, he started up once with this "everyone just wants something from you when you're rich," shit. It's what the cool kids these days call a humblebrag. And I knew exactly what he was doing. Bragging about being rich. I'm not fucking stupid. On the contrary, I'm probably one of the smartest people in the world, and that is *not* a humblebrag, that's merely a fact. And if you're offended by facts, it's probably because you're a Science damn conservative!

Once, when he was going on and on about how he doesn't really have any true friends, because it always comes around to what he could do for anyone he was trying to befriend, I offered to help him. "Look," I told him. "I'm a yacht builder. I build yachts out of wood, by hand, over here on my property. That's why I have all the sheds." And can you believe, come to think back on that time, that he said, "oh, I thought you were just a hoarder." That mother fucker! And to think, I was trying to help him!

Anyway, I kept on, overlooking his comment as maybe he was just still drunk and not really in full control of what he was saying, and I said, "look. Why don't you just buy a yacht from me? We'll take it out on the water, get to know each other, and maybe we'll become friends."

"Where in the fuck are we going to go yachting around here?" he asked, like I was supposed to fall for *that*.

"We don't have to go around here," I told him. "We'll take it out wherever you've got your other yachts moored. Down on the Chesapeake Bay somewhere. Or down at the Outer Banks."

He started laughing so hard he almost pissed himself. "You think I have a fucking yacht moored down at the beach?" he said, and he just kept laughing.

"Of *course* you do," I told him.

"What in the hell makes you think I've got a yacht moored up down at the beach?"

"Because you're fucking rich!" I told him. "All you fucking rich people have yachts moored up down at the Bay, or the beach, or down at the Outer Banks. Hell, probably over at Lake Anna."

"You're a hoot," he told me. "I think I *could* be friends with a guy like you."

"Great!" I said. "I'm working on a yacht now. I've run out of funds to finish it (because at that time, and with that yacht, I had), but you can just prepay me for the finished product and that way I'll be able to buy the supplies I need and then get the boat complete. I'll knock ten per cent off the final price since you'll have to wait about six months for me to finish."

Then, this crazy rich bastard looks at me, all straight faced and shit and says, "you're serious, aren't you?"

I told him *of course* I was serious.

He looked at me and said, "see. You're just like everyone else. Trying to figure out how to benefit from my existence. All I am is a fucking ATM machine to you people. And all I ever do is give, give, and give some more."

And then he turned and walked off into the woods. As a matter of fact, it was after that time that he really started passing out drunk on my property *way* less. Somehow, even while in his drunken stupors he'd manage to give my place a wide berth. Oh well, fuck him. He was lying to me anyway. I know he's got a yacht somewhere. All these crazy rich people have yachts. But their yachts are not as good as my yachts. I was just trying to give him a better quality product, save him money, and who knows, maybe become his friend, which he obviously wanted, as much as he's always crying about how 'everyone only wants you for what you can do for them when you're rich.'

Anyway, I know you've been wondering about the crazy old rich guy that stays drunk in the woods behind my house, so there you have it.

Now, on to that bitch ex-wife of mine.

...wait.

I think that crazy rich Asian guy next door is actually coming outside.

Yeah, I came out here to my storage shed to get something. I can't remember what. But I just happened to be looking over there at the perfect time. I can see the whole fucking house from here since I felled that tree a couple years back. From the side view, of course, but like I said, it allows me to see the front porch *and* the back porch.

Damn it! I don't have my binoculars, so I can't tell from this distance if that's him or that Asian whore of his. Whichever one it is, they're in a white robe, and they're on the *back* porch.

Holy shit!

It's him!

How do I know? Because he's *standing* there *pissing* off his back porch! Science damn! You can take the peasant out of the third world country, but you can't take the third world country out of the peasant!

Son of a bitch! Doesn't he know he's got indoor plumbing now?

But hey, at least the crazy lunatic bastard finally came outside.

6

Okay, so back to that bitch of an ex-wife of mine.

She totally used me and then left me just before she was going to start drawing from her pension and inherit her rich parents' money, and boy did she make sure to kick me in the pride while I was down.

How?

By giving me the fucking house and everything in it without even contesting it. Can you believe that?

What *audacity* and what *arrogance*!

And that just goes to prove why I hate rich people. I mean, she wasn't rich at the time, but she was getting ready to be rich, because her parents were rich, and I think they'd actually threatened to take her out of their will if she didn't leave me. I believe they'd been threatening that for years. Always calling me a deadbeat. Just because I work for myself and build yachts instead of having a job, maybe, for a ship building company, and using my skills to make someone else rich. All you have to do to find out I'm no deadbeat is go into any of my storage sheds out back and look at all my supplies and equipment. Have a look at the beautiful and nearly completed hull of the yacht I'm currently working on!

Anyway, my ex-wife stayed with me for the longest time, because she didn't care about money any more than I ever did, but I guess she started seeing dollar signs, and after she'd placed her parents in a long term care facility she really started thinking about all that money she was going to get soon, if she left me, of course, so she left me. I guess she knew that if her parents were in that place, they were on their final leg, so she'd better hurry up and get rid of me before they checked out so she could get all that money. Maybe they'd already written her out of the will and she was trying to hurry up and get written back in. I don't know.

I tried my best to talk her into staying, but she had some standard bullshit go-to phrase she'd say over and over and then just walk out. She told me that it was obvious that she wasn't able to give me what I needed. What the hell does that even mean? She should have just said, "it's not you, it's me." I mean, both statements are equally meaningless.

Anyway, I guess we knew each other as kids, but I'd forgotten her. After my first divorce I'd been asked by my old shop teacher from high school to come in and give a demonstration on the wood lathe, because he knew I was the best wood turner there was. He used to tell me that in high school, and it's as true today as it was back then. I mean, I always thought that colored kid I told you about earlier was just as good, but our teacher was white, so, well, you know the rest.

Anyway, it turns out my ex-wife- this is wife number two, mind you, we're talking about here- was a teacher, and she was teaching at our old high school. She recognized me, but again, I didn't recognize her. Honestly, to this day I do *not* remember her from school. Probably because she's very unremarkable, which, of course, would make her very unmemorable.

Hey, I'm not trying to be mean, it's just true. I didn't marry her for her looks, okay? I married her because we were like-minded. She didn't care about money. I mean, hell. She was a *teacher* for Science-sake. And she didn't ask to be brought up in a rich family. She didn't ask to be born into it. She didn't bitch and cry about it, like the crazy rich drunk bastard in the woods out back.

When she told me who her parents were, I certainly remembered them. They're, like, local legends in a way. Her father was one of the richest bastards around here, and he was always donating money here, donating money there, and I *knew* he did it just to get his name put on buildings and shit, the fucking narcicist. The man's name is on half the shit in the county, because he's the one who gave them the money to build the buildings, whoever *they* were. Battered women and children facilities, children's hospitals, animal shelters, various youth athletic complexes. And that arrogant bastard's name went up on all of them. They might not have named the damn places after him, but sure enough they put a huge bronze plaque up on the front of them all which clearly stated the funds for the project were made available by him.

Anyway, as it happened, my ex-wife- number two here- had just gone through a divorce herself. Her first husband, the father of her two kids- (and let me tell you, they're nothing worth looking at, either- a boy and a girl- and I *always* made sure to let anyone we met know they were *not* my kids- no way, huh-uh!) was a cop, and I guess he'd been fucking around on her all over town pretty much. He was a good looking guy. Ex-military. Total bitch magnet. And it was apparent he'd just married her for her parents' money, anyway. So he got what he deserved when he got the boot. Sure, he stuck with his career, and he's making good money as a cop now that he is in his final, high income earning years. And he always provided health insurance for his kids and paid child support, and just did all the right things the right way. Oh, and he'll get a hell of a nice pension when he retires, since he is a Government worker and whatnot. Oh, he'll be set, financially, but not like he would have been if he hadn't fucked up and gotten the boot by our now mutual ex-wife. He would have been living in the lap of luxury, as I would have been, but it looks like maybe that conniving bitch was able to pull the wool over *both* our eyes. Oh well, he's not rich, but I still hate him. And since he's a cop and ex-military and all that, I'm sure he's probably one of those asshole conservatives, anyway. Gee, I wonder how many unarmed black men *he's* gotten away with killing in the line of duty?

But back to her.

The long and short of it is that once I'd found out she was single I decided I'd mercy date her. I mean, she was a single mom with two kids now, trying to live off of a teacher's salary (well, and mommy and daddy's money), so I was really doing her a favor. And yet, all those years later, that bitch up and left me just before she started drawing from her teacher's pension, and just so she could get mommy and daddy's money. I had *no clue* she was so greedy. I mean, like her pension wasn't enough? She had to get an inheritance, too? And to tell me to just take the house, because she didn't want to deal with fighting me over it? And to tell me it was obvious that she couldn't give me what I needed?

I needed that fucking pension money!

And her fucking inheritance!

Whatever.

Since I'm not greedy, and I don't need much, I'm just going to start drawing my social security as early as possible. When I'm sixty two. Only...

...wait a minute...

...I see that little Asian whore leaving the house next door!

Wow, so I guess he came out and took a piss off the porch after he was done nailing her, and she got all whored up and ready to go somewhere. I'll be damned if she's not going somewhere. She's getting in that little BMW of hers that she's no doubt bought with the money she's earned spreading those sexy little brown legs of hers. Oh, and she's wearing her typical little microskirt. Damn, I'd love to take a peek up one of her little skirts someday.

And I guess the crazy fucking rich Asian bastard's going to just lay around and sleep all day. Science knows he's not going anywhere. Just sleep all day and wait for one of his call girls to come back. Maybe wake up and roll out of bed long enough to make a few grand by clicking the mouse button on a stock trade or two.

I personally would never trust the stock market. It's run by rich crooks- Jews and Capitalists- but I bet that's what that guy does all day. Sits in there and trades stocks. You know, I've heard Asians are good at math, and that's all finances are, really. Math.

No, I'm not stereotyping with anything I just said! I'm a progressive…

…we've already covered this!

Anyway, my ex-wife was leaving just around the time that Nazi and his mail order bride that used to live next door were moving in. I guess there's a silver lining to all gray clouds. You see, my stepson had just turned eighteen- he went to live with his mother, of course, when she left me- and my step daughter didn't like her mother much so she was living with her father and she had been for years, already, by the time her mother left me- but anyway, the silver lining is that my step son got out of here just before he probably would have done something stupid, like hit his rich grandparents up for enough money to go over there and have paid for sex with that Nazi guy's mail order bride. It wasn't long before they'd moved in over there that his mother had obviously discovered a long, much watched history of pornography on our computer. She'd done a history search. Checked the cookies and all that shit. Hours upon hours of porn. She asked me about it, and I said, hey, he *is* a teenager. It's what they do. Eat junk food and jack off.

She told me she'd never talked to him about it, but I could tell she wasn't comfortable with it. We never went into detail about what he was looking at, because, well, that's just gross. But have you seen some of the shit on the internet? Like shit with animals? I'm telling you, that crazy rich fucker with the camel? I bet he's on the internet doing something with that animal, if not others, somewhere. I bet if a person were to look hard enough.

Anyway, back to the situation. She at least got her porn addicted kid out of here just in time, because you know that if he would have had the money, he could have had that little whore that was just moving in next door right when he was leaving. I mean, come on. Everyone knows those girls just marry these lonely old white guys to get to America, and then they leave them for someone their own age once they get here. And she looked like she was the same age as my step son, even though I'm sure she was older. Asian women just age really well.

But at least my ex-wife got to do one last good deed around here before she left me. I told you, she and I were like-minded, I used to think about everything, but I guess in the end, not about money. But when it comes to social justice and responsibility? Well, let me tell you, the minute she looked over there and saw that young little Asian mail order bride with that middle aged white man, she marched right over there and did a social health and welfare check. She made sure to let that girl know that men are *not* allowed to beat women in this country, and she gave her the phone number and address of the battered women and children's facility downtown. I have to hand it to her, that was one hell of a good thing for her to do before leaving.

Selfish fucking bitch!

7

You know, since we're on the topic, I want to let you know, all I ever tried to do was be friends with that guy next door. No, not that crazy sex addicted lunatic Asian guy who's living over there now and who's either running a whorehouse or is day trading. But speaking of him, I actually saw him come out of his house again a couple of days ago.

Yeah, I might have been over there at that one spot beside my outbuildings where I keep my materials and the hull of the yacht I'm currently building just trying to get a sneak peek of that little Asian girl he's hooked up with over there. I'd seen her come home in her little Beemer the night before, so I knew she'd be leaving the next morning, because she's pretty regular with her schedule, and…

…okay, I'll admit it. She's hot as hell, and I guess I kind of have a thing for her, and I know what time she usually leaves, and I was hoping to get just a glimpse of her in her little skirt I knew she'd be wearing. She's *always* wearing those little skirts, and, well, what I wouldn't give to get a glimpse up one of them some day.

Just once!

Anyway, she was running late. She hadn't left yet. And sure enough, while I'm watching the house, that crazy fucking Asian guy comes out the back door again, in that white robe he's always wearing, and he takes a freaking piss off of the porch again. Well, I was getting pretty pissed (that's my shitty attempt at a pun, and I do *not* apologize, because I *never* apologize), and I was thinking about going over there and telling him to use the fucking indoor plumbing, because he's not in Cambodia anymore, or wherever the hell he's from, because if he keeps doing that, I'm eventually going to be able to smell the stench of it all the way over here, and just about that time, he looks over, and I could tell he saw me.

Well, I bent over and picked up a stick, trying to make it look like I was just out clearing up my yard- which I never do, and which is part of the story I was starting to tell you before I got sidetracked with this one- well, anyway, he freaking smiled really big, turned to face me, and then he started shaking that thing around, almost as if to say, "come and get it!"

Okay, so everyone knows Asians are supposed to be hung like gnats, right? Well not *this* guy. He was hung like a fucking mule, and all of a sudden I completely understood why he had two whores instead of just one. Damn, if I had a piece like that, I'd want to use it as much as I could, too…

…okay.

I'm sorry.

This was not supposed to be about my crazy Asian neighbor's penis.

But anyway, he put that thing back inside his robe and went back inside the house, and it was damn near another hour before that little Asian whore that's with him over there came out in her tiny little skirt and got in her Beemer and went wherever the hell she goes during the day. To service other clients, I'm sure. But I guess after he pissed he went right back inside and gave it to her again. Must be why she was in there another hour. I sure as hell wouldn't want to be her next customer after she got railed by that monster for almost an hour. Talk about *super* sloppy seconds!

Anyway, back to what I was trying to get at in the first place; that right winged Nazi that used to rent over there before the old woman who owned the house died off and her no good greedy simply waiting around on her to die kids inherited the house and sold it to that Asian pimp day trader. All I ever tried to do was be his friend. That's what I was starting to tell you.

So I guess he'd been in the Marines or some shit. Maybe the Army. I don't know. But when I first met him he mentioned he was in Iraq. And he was talking about some military shit. I told him, yeah, yeah, I remember that from when I was in the Navy.

Well, with that, this guy lit up like a Christmas tree. And I knew he would. It's that whole 'band of brothers' thing, you know. People who have served in the military have all been through something that most people could never imagine. No matter how else they might differ in life, they have that connection.

Anyway, he'd always bring up his Army days, or Marines, or whatever, and he'd talk about when he was in Afghanistan- maybe it was Iraq- I can't remember, but one of those Middle Eastern shitholes that is suffering because of America. I tell you, I'm not willing to go live in some third world shithole, because I'm comfortable here, but if you think for a minute that I love my country, you, Ma'am and Sir, are sadly mistaken. We have caused more pain and suffering on this planet than any single nation before or since us, and if you ask me, we owe the whole fucking world an apology!

So, one day I see that Nazi over there mowing his grass- oh, and that's a whole other story- he fucking kept that place looking like a resort, and he was fucking renting! I told him he was crazy spending all that time keeping the place looking like that, but he said some shit about self respect or dignity or some shit. Let me tell you, anyone who has *any* self respect or dignity does *not* do yard work. Hell, *any* kind of manual labor for that matter.

And I hear you, you're like, "but I thought you built yachts. Isn't that a form of manual labor?" Well of *course* there's manual labor *involved*. But I don't do *that* part. I *hire* people to do that part. I'm the brains, they're the backs. And yard work? Seriously? Hey, I am socially conscious and progressive, so when I need yard work done, I hire immigrants. It's why they come here in the first place, and it's our responsibility to help them by letting them do the work they came here to do. Anyone who takes care of their own lawn is merely taking a job away from a Latin American immigrant, the greedy, xoenophobic bastards!

Anyway, that Nazi was over there mowing on this super hot day, and I go over there, and he stops mowing and starts talking to me, and somehow, basic training comes up. He's talking about how hot it was in Ft. Benning, Georgia in July, because that's when he was there in basic training. Must have been Army then. I don't know. Maybe Marines. Maybe he said Ft. Lejeune down in North Carolina. Somewhere farther south of here where it gets really, really hot.

So this guy, all of a sudden, asks me about basic training in the Navy. He said he'd heard the Navy does basic training on one of the Great Lakes. "Yeah," I told him. "Lake Michigan." Well, that wasn't good enough for him. He starts pressing me. He asked me what that was like, doing basic training on one of the Great Lakes. Wants to know if I did it in the summer or if I had the great displeasure of going in the winter. I told him that I didn't go to basic training.

"Oh," he says. "So you did ROTC and went straight into the Navy as an officer?"

"Kinda," I said.

"What does 'kinda' mean?" he asks. What a fucking asshole, right? Like he's now interrogating me. Most people just thank you for your service when you tell them you're a veteran and leave it at that. I mean, they know it's disrespectful to press for specifics. They don't know what kind of shit you might have been through.

"Well," I told him, "I wasn't *officially* in the Navy. I was in ROTC in college, and *technically* it's the same thing."

Man, did that piss him off! He came flying off that riding lawn mower like he was ready to fight.

"You mean you're not a fucking veteran?" he says.

"Well," I tell him again, because the dumbass obviously didn't hear me the first time, "*officially*, no, but I was in ROTC in college, and *technically* it's the same thing as being in the Navy, because our ROTC instructor was a Naval officer, and we had to do the same shit." And I told him all about it. I mean, once a month we had to go spend a weekend in the field. Do you know how hard that shit was? I mean, our ROTC campground was on the side of a hill up above the football stadium, and in the fall, we'd have to sit up there in the woods and listen to the game, wishing we were there, but knowing we couldn't be, because we'd made a commitment to our country. And I told that Nazi nextdoor this, and that just seemed to piss him off even more!

"Look," he says, and you could tell he was trying to keep from exploding. I mean, you talk about a lunatic, this guy was a fucking lunatic. He had the *audacity* to go on and tell me that he wasn't going to punch me in the throat, because we were neighbors, but that I needed to stop telling people I'd served in the Navy and acting like I'm a veteran, because I didn't and I wasn't. He told me if I got caught up in that by a real veteran, or someone who respected veterans and who wasn't my neighbor, I'd get punched in the throat. What a fucking idiot. I've been telling people I was in the Navy for the last thirty years and I've *never* come *close* to getting punched in the throat or anywhere else.

Being in ROTC in college and being in the actual military is the same damn thing, and everyone knows it, and this guy- this Nazi- he knew it, too, and he was just jealous, because he was an enlisted man, I'm sure- I mean, I could tell by how dumb he was- and he knew that if I'd actually gone into the

Navy I would have gone in as an officer, because I'd done ROTC in college. He knew I would have had higher pay and I would have received more respect. And it just pissed him off.

And another thing. He was just one of those dumb Army guys. I don't know, maybe one of those dumb Marine guys. Either way, he knows those of us who go Navy or Airforce are way smarter than those dumbasses that join the Army or the Marines. I mean, don't get me wrong. The Army and the Marines are perfect for young black men whose fathers are in prison, if they even know who their fathers are in the first place. You know, these inner city blacks that grow up without discipline or any sort of structure? The Army and the Marines are both great places for those guys. It could make the difference between a good military career or a life spent in and out of prison, which is pretty much what all those guys are going to end up going through at some point or another, anyway. It's just a matter of time.

Hey, I'm just being statistically correct here, not racist. I'm a progressive liberal who used to vote Democrat, so it's not even *possible* for me to be racist. We've covered this a dozen times already. Sure, I'm a white male, and I feel guilty as hell about it, but I'm just saying. Don't put words in my mouth. I'm statistically profiling, not racially profiling. Numbers mean something.

Whatever, I waved it off and said just that. "Whatever!" and I told him I didn't want to keep him from his beloved yard work, and I left. Oh, don't you worry. I got him back. I got him back good, and it has to do with beloved yard work. Mine, not his. But…

…wait a minute…

...I see a car coming...

...let me grab my binoculars...

...oh, my God! It's the Asian whore and the blonde from across the way. Man, that crazy fucking Asian lunatic guy is going to be putting that giant snake to use tonight!

8

Well, I was out there this morning trying to get a look at that Asian whore again, and I guess I missed her. Her Beemer was already gone. I got out a little later than usual, because I'd slept in later than usual. I was up late down in the basement working on my yacht, and, well, sometimes when I'm working at night, I'll have a beer or six, and sometimes I just get caught up in my work and the beer, and well, then I'll have twelve or fifteen, and well, the next day I just don't get up as early as I usually do, and today was one of those days, so I missed her. Oh well, maybe I'll see her when she comes home, and I got a pretty good show, late getting outside as I was, anyway.

No, I didn't get to see the Asian daytrading pimp lunatic's monster snake again. I got to see a nearly five hundred pound fat ass bastard hauled out of his house dead!

I know that sounds sick, and I'm not trying to be mean. I'm nice. I don't make fun of people for being fat or retarded or anything. Everybody gets a free serving of nice with me, just like when they order Domino's Pizza. I'm a progressive liberal who used to vote Democrat, and even though I don't vote anymore, I *am* on board the nice wagon the Dems have going on these days. But listen, this fat bastard literally weighed five hundred pounds! The only person I've ever seen even close to being that big was his asshole son who died about six months ago. He was over four hundred pounds. I actually got to see that fat bastard drop dead! Hauled his ass off in an ambulance, but hell, he was already dead. They never brought him back, so what's that tell you?

Okay, so from my little vantage point out there by the shed where I keep the hull of the yacht I'm currently working on…

…what's that? You thought it was in the basement, because I was in there working on it so late last night?

No, silly. That's just where I do the computer stuff. The planning. Besides, I've already explained I don't do any of the actual labor. It's beneath me. I was born of a special metal. I am truly an elitist, intellectually, and it's by birth. It's a good thing I got out of politics years ago, or I probably would have become president, and I'd fix this fucked up country. I'd start by deporting all these Nazis, like the one that used to live next door, back to Germany!

Okay, so from that vantage point, I can see out across the lunatic Asian daytrading pimp neighbor's place, and I can see where the little blonde whore he's fucking lives, and I can see the house beside that one. And now you talk about true lunatics, that's who lives there. Well, that's who *used* to live there. Not now. They're all dead. And because I was out there this morning, I got to see them haul that whale of a fat bastard last one of them out. And would you believe that for as long as

I've lived here, that was the absolute first time I'd ever seen him?

I shit you not!

And the first time I saw his wife was just about a month ago. They brought her out on a pallet, because she was well over three hundred pounds. And, I mean, technically, even then, when they hauled them out with a forklift- oh yes, just wait, I'm going to tell you all about it- but even then I didn't actually see them, because they had them covered. That's how I knew they were dead. You know how they cover you with a sheet when you die and all that? And they were both so big, they didn't haul them off in ambulances, because they wouldn't fit. They loaded them up into these big white box trucks. And they had to take part of the wall off of the side of the house, right there by the door frame, to get them out, they were that fucking huge!

The old man and old woman were both agoraphobes. Never left the house. Kinda like that batshit crazy Asian daytrading pimp living over there beside me now. What is it about this place? I mean, I hardly ever go out, during the day especially, because of the sun, and I already told you big pharma's not milking me out of what money I *do* have for cancer treatments just to let me die once the money's gone. But these people? I mean, that Asian freak- and I'm not saying that because he's Asian, but because he's a freak- he doesn't even seem to go out at night, unless I'm sleeping and miss it.

So anyway, let me tell you about these fat bastards. Well, at least their son, because like I said, mom and dad never left the house until they died. Can you believe they had to put them on some kind of specially built litter and then drag them to the door and transfer them to a pallet and then pick them up and lift them through the door with a forklift? Well, through the door and the part of the wall they had to remove beside the door frame just to be able to get them out of the house. It was a hell of a scene. I'm glad I always keep my binoculars out there under the awning of my outbuilding so I'm able to see this kind of stuff when it happens.

Well, the son was a real lunatic and a bully on top of that. I never had to deal with him, because most of my property is wooded. There's just one tiny patch of grass down close to where it borders the crazy Asian daytrading pimp guy's property, and I just let it go fallow. I've been a little lighter in the wallet since that bitch of an ex-wife of mine left me and took away this household's second income- not to mention soon to be pension and inheritance- so I've not been able to hire these immigrant guys I used to hire to weed for me down there.

They are from Guatemala, these immigrant guys I'd hire to do my shit work. I used to use them to test people, too, to find out if they were racist or not. I'd have someone over, and this was a long time ago- and it was always my ex-wife's friends who were over- but I'd say to them, 'look out there at my Mexican workers. Aren't they doing a good job?' And they'd always look out and see the guys working, and then they'd smile and say, 'yeah, it looks great,' and then they'd go right back to talking to my ex-wife, like I wasn't even there. Well, once they left, I'd tell my ex-wife that her racist friends were not welcome in my house again. She'd ask me what I meant, racist, and I told her. I said I'd asked her friends if they thought my Mexican workers were doing a good job, and they'd said yes.

They weren't fucking Mexican! They were Guatemalan! And my ex-wife's friends obviously thought that everyone from south of the border is Mexican, or that all people of Latin descent look the same.

Hey, that might be true with Asians, especially Southeast Asians. I mean, they have all those tiny little countries over there, smaller than most of our states, and all the different types of Asians living in those tiny countries, like Malaysians, Singaporians, Indonesians, Filipinos, and they all pretty much look the same, because, and I mean, let's face it, they pretty much *are* the same- they're all just divided by some water- and somehow, we're supposed to be able to tell a difference between them all? I mean, I've never been to Southeast Asia, hell, I've never been out of the U.S., but I watch National Geographic, so I know what I'm talking about. I stay informed, just like any *true* progressive.

Anyway, it's not like that, at all, with Latino's, so I didn't want those racist bastards back in *this* house. They were *not* welcome in this house. I am progressive and socially conscious and no one who is not the same is welcome in my home. And I told my wife, well, my ex-wife, that she was *not* to frequent the homes of racist Nazis. I didn't care how long she'd known some of them.

Anyway, those two had a fat bastard son, and boy, was he a piece of work. Look, I said all my crazy neighbors are rich, and we all know that all rich people are crazy, but those bastards- the family of fat bastards- they weren't rich. There simply was no way they could have been. Why, if you could see their property? It looks like a damn landfill! I have no idea how they even acquired their place out here in the first place. I mean, it's pricey out here. The only thing I can think of is maybe they've been out here for generations, just having land handed down to them, one generation after another.

You know, there used to be an estate tax to redistribute the wealth in this country, as it should be, because how is it fair that the crazy rich drunk bastard that lives out behind me gets to just drink beer all day everyday and whine (another cheep pun intended, and you should know by now I never apologize) about his Daddy issues, and he can afford to do it because someone in his family a few generations back did something with their lives, but a guy like me, I have to slave over my work while I drink my beer, like last night down in the basement. If I don't earn, I don't drink. Hell, I drink Natural Light as it is, because I can get a fifteen pack for ten dollars. Boy, there's a story for you.

The asshole clerk where I get my beer when I go out twice a week for provisions- never between the hours of 1 p.m. and 4 p.m., mind you, and usually at night- always laughs and tells me that I'm the only person he knows who isn't in their twenties that drinks Natty Light. Since I'm in my fifties, I guess I'm supposed to be drinking those high octane I.P.A.s or something. Hey, they might be high octane, but they're high priced, too, and not all of us are rich. That clerk is a college student down at the University, no doubt. I'm sure he is. I don't even know why he's working. All those kids that go to that University are rich. I mean, I went there, and I'm not rich, but my father worked there, contract construction work off and on, so he pulled strings and I qualified for a shitton of aid. I thought it was great at first, until I actually went to school with all those rich snobs. Boy, if there's anyone who has a right to hate rich people, it's me, let me tell you.

Anyway, I guess those fat bastards were living out here because someone somewhere in their past lineage worked, but by God *they* sure didn't. That fatass son of theirs had a dozen cows or so over there, and they didn't have enough land to run cows on *and* to grow enough hay to feed them in the winter on, because of that estate tax thing we used to have before that bastard that was in office a few years back removed it. He was a Republican, so he was just helping all his rich friends. But you see, when we had the estate tax, you pretty much had to sell anything of value past the point of a million dollars or so to pay the estate taxes upon inheritance. And it made the world a better place.

For example, those fat bastards- the parents- I'm sure they used to own the land the blonde whore's house is on, but when their fat bastard parents died they had to sell half of their total land holding to pay the estate taxes on it all. So, over several generations of fat bastards dying off, you could easily see a property the size of a thousand acres diminished to a hundred or less. And that's how it should *still* be, because why should someone benefit just from being lucky enough to be born into the right family, and a guy like me, who's smarter than anyone you've ever met, have to fucking work just to make enough money to buy cheep beer, and then, only to be laughed at for it from some snobby rich kid who was lucky enough to be born into the right family?

Okay, so anyway, this fat kid of theirs would bully everyone who lived around here who had properties even of just an acre or two- but of course, he prefered them bigger- he would bully them into letting him cut their grass in order to use it as hay. I guess everyone was scared of him, because he was so big, so they just let him do it.

So, like the homo queer with the camel, for instance. You know, the camel breeding bastard- and no, I don't mean as in animal husbandry, either- I mean as in I think he's breeding with the camel! Have you seen some of the sick shit on the internet? Someone's making that shit, and I think he's one of those someones!

Anyway, camel guy has about ten acres. The big fat bully cut about eight of it for his hay. I guess he was kind enough to let the camel keep two acres of grass for food, but that was it. The fat bastard took the rest. Man, was that fat bastard a bully.

As it turned out, the fatass bully bastard of a son of theirs had a dozen or so of these neighbors around here giving him hay, and he was just waiting for his parents to die, I guess, so he'd get the house and the land- he was about my age, I guess, and he was still living at home- and look at the irony of it all. The fat bastard ended up dying before his parents. Hell, now that they're all gone, I don't know *what's* going to happen to that place.

I wouldn't take it if you gave it to me. You talk about hoarders. They've got old cars and tractors- yes, mostly old tractors- just piled up so thick behind the house, at least from what I can see from my seeing place. I mean, I've never gone over there, but it looks like a fucking landfill from here. I mean, it would take someone who bought the property more money than the property is worth to have all that shit hauled away. I don't know if the guy used all those old tractors for parts or what, but my Science, you've never *seen* so many tractors. Old as hell, too.

Anyway, if you want to know how he died, he was out there weed eating under his electric fencing and he just dropped dead. Guess his heart just couldn't take pumping the blood through all the blubber anymore. And I saw that shit. I was out there watching the whole thing through my binoculars from my seeing place. Hell, if I hadn't known any better, I would have thought he saw me watching. Looked at first like he was mouthing the word 'help' over and over again. Like, "help. Help." Fuck him. He should have eaten less twinkies. He somehow managed to pull his phone out of his pocket and dial 911, because an ambulance came screaming through about twenty minutes later, but like I said, he must have died on the way to the hospital or once he got there, because he hasn't come back.

And then, a few months later, his mom goes, and now his dad. Hell, who knows who'll get the house and land now? Hopefully the Government seizes it and gives it to someone who deserves it.

Anyway, I've gotta get out there to the outbuilding. It's about time for that little Asian whore to come over and service her mule hung stud. I'm telling you, she is so good to look at, and if it's my dying wish, I'm gonna get a look up her skirt someday.

By the way, I'm thinking about maybe going over there to Asia and buying me one of those mail order brides. As soon as I sell the yacht I'm currently working on. I've been going through a dry spell, and I can't afford to make the minimum payments on my credit cards right now. Things were a lot easier when my ex-wife was still here, because even though she didn't make much, being a teacher and all, she at least made something, and I could at least keep the credit rolling, because

I was making payments, so when I'd go through a dry spell, I could always just get another credit card or open another line of credit somewhere. But she's not here, so my credit's taken a hit, and I've not been able to find a buyer for the yacht I'm currently working on, so I can't just run off to Asia and buy me a little mail order bride like that Nazi lunatic that used to live next door did. I mean, I'm not trying to sound like I'm stereotyping here, but come on. Why would a beautiful, young, sexy Asian girl like that Nazi's wife be with an older white guy, hell, old enough to be her dad, if it *wasn't* about the money? I mean, I'd never come right out and say that, because I'm a progressive liberal, and I used to vote Democrat, and you'd better believe I'm all about cultural sensitivity, but I'm coming right out and saying it, I guess.

Okay, I'll keep you updated. I've got to go get my sneak peek...

...oh, shit...

...I hear her car crushing gravel on the driveway.

Gotta go!

Just when I thought that crazy, sex addicted, day trading lunatic Asian pimp nextdoor couldn't be any more insane, I found out I was wrong.

Way wrong!

You are *not* going to believe this!

So yesterday evening, when I went out there to see if I could get a peek of that little Asian whore girlfriend of his, I got a peek of a whole lot more than that! Sure, I saw her pulling up in her Beemer, but I didn't get to peek up her microskirt. But let me tell you what I *did* see, and it was no less interest grabbing.

So she pulls up and parks, and before she even gets out, this freaking guy gets out of the passenger side of the car. And let me tell you, this guy was freaking hot! I mean, as far as guys go, you know what I mean? He resembled that guy that plays Captain America. Chris somebody. Blond hair, I'm assuming blue eyes- I mean, my binoculars are pretty strong, but they're not *that* damn strong- and man, he was built like a linebacker.

But that's not all! So, he gets out, then the little Asian whore gets out, and they meet up at the back of the car, before going inside, and they start freaking kissing! And dude reaches around and grabs her on that little round and brown ass of hers and squeezes it so hard I could hear her squeal from over *here!*

But that's *still* not all! Next thing you know, that little blonde whore from across the way pulls up in her BMW. She gets out and walks up to them, and they all do this group hug and kiss thing, and then they go inside, and that was the last I saw of them until this morning, and that's an even *better* story. Wait until I get to *that* part.

Now, yesterday evening, I thought at first my eyes were deceiving me. I mean, from what I saw, from my little vantage point out there by the shed where I keep the completely finished (well, almost) hull of the yacht I'm currently building, and through the lenses of the best military grade binoculars approved for civilian use money can buy (and I know, because, as *you* know, I used to be in R.O.T.C., which is pretty much the same thing as the military) I clearly saw what looked like what was well on the way of becoming one of those bisexual orgy sexapades!

If you think I'm nuts, then you haven't spent enough time on the internet, and you don't know enough about these damn millennials. They don't recognize the same boundaries we did when we were younger and that we still do today. I mean, pretty much, they do what they want, and they don't give a Science-damn about what other people think about it.

Millennials are living together for years without getting married, even if they have children together. Sometimes multiple children! Hey, I read about it on the internet. They said they knew that the generations before them all got married because they got pregnant, and they wanted to do the right thing. Well, these millennials were the products of those unplanned pregnancies and the shotgun weddings that followed, and they all sat back as children and watched their parents and grandparents go through selfish divorces- that's their words, not mine- selfish divorces that ruined their childhoods, and they say they're not going to do it to *their* children. They say that if the time is ever right to get married for the right reasons, they will, but until then, they're just as content to cohabitate and have multiple children out of wedlock until the cows come home.

Oh, and they like to have a bunch of bisexial orgy sexapades.

Now listen, don't get me wrong. I'm not pushing morals here. I can assure you, I am no Christian. Jeesh, talk about a bunch of ignorant fucks. I mean, evolution is pretty clear. But I also want to point out, let's not start bashing people of faith from other religions, just because I'm not a Christian. Not all Muslims are terrorists, and not all terrorists are Muslims. I mean, just look at that Nazi bastard that used to live nextdoor to me. I can see him in the papers some day, shooting someone for being gay, or Muslim, or black, or… whatever, anything other than white, straight and Christian. You'll never see *me* ending up like that, because I'm progressive and tolerant. But I'm just not cutting any slack for these Christian bastards. Every conflict that has nearly decimated mankind as a whole can be traced back to their bloody crusades. And when these self-proclaimed patriots scream about how America was built on Christian values, I agree with them. You're damn right it was. That's why it's so fucked up!

Anyway, I was up all night trying to convince myself that I had not just witnessed what I had clearly just witnessed. There is no way these four good looking young millennials were going to be in there all night having a foursome. But I ended up getting two more pieces of proof!

Okay, piece of proof number one; later that night, well after dark, I was hanging out out there by my shed just trying to see if I could hear anything. I was drinking some Natty Light, because it was a warm evening, and I'd been down in the basement all day working on my yacht. You know, the schematic parts of it. We've already discussed the labor part. I don't do it. I know the type of metal of which I was born, and it ain't bronze, let me tell you.

So I hear the front door open over there, and I look over and see light flooding onto the front porch from within the house. The blonde bimbo from across the way comes out of the house, and then Captain America and the little Asian whore step out into the dim light being cast out onto the porch from inside the house with her. The blonde whore says she had a great time, and that she was worn out, and that they all needed to get together and do it again sometime. Captain America said he was up for it whenever she was. Then, I heard the crazy Asian day trading pimp lunatic say he was up for it anytime again, too. He must have been just inside the door, because he hadn't joined them on the porch, but I clearly heard his voice.

Okay, so I stayed up all night drinking, convincing myself that I'd merely witnessed a group of friends getting together for game night, right? I mean, my ex-wife, number two we're talking about here, was always trying to get me to go to game night with other couples she knew. She roped me into it one time. I went to game night with her and some douchebag therapist named Byron Blevins who lives not far from us, actually, and some other guy that was hanging out with him. I can't remember the other guy's name. I didn't care enough to remember it then, so I don't care enough to remember now, but that whole get together was all a setup. Oh, I'll get into that later. But for now, I've got to tell you about this.

So, I'm up all night, drinking Natty Light, and doing some work on the computer, trying to convince myself I hadn't seen what I'd seen, but I got all of the evidence I needed just this morning. Just a little while ago.

Okay, I've already admitted it. Sometimes I drink way too much Natty Light, and I know I'm probably self medicating my insomnia. When the insomnia monster comes at me, he stays here for weeks at a time. I mean, I've got so much to worry about, and that's another thing that pissed me off about that Nazi that used to live next door. I told him once about how I'd been up at three in the morning, fighting insomnia, and of how it was kind of neat that particular time, because it was during the fireflies' peak of mating season, so it was like looking out the window and seeing mother nature's light show. You know what that son of a bitch said to me? He said, "yeah, I've suffered from insomnia ever since getting back from Iraq, what caused yours?" I mean, he might have said Afghanistan, I don't really know where he was. I didn't care enough to remember when he used to tell me, and I sure don't care enough to remember now. But anyway, what audacity! Like I have to have a reason to have insomnia, and like it's got to be comparable to combat. At the time, he still believed I'd served in the Navy, so I told him I didn't want to talk about it, and he gave me the respect I'm deserving of and didn't push it. Unlike that time a couple months later when he pushed me on that basic training bullshit and I went ahead and outed myself for having never served.

Anyway, let me tell you why I have insomnia. Okay, I'm like, two hundred miles away from the ocean, but let me tell you, within one lifetime, my front yard is going to be oceanfront property! Why? Because of global warming, that's why! I mean, if it's not even safe to go outside into the sun as a human being, what's that say about the plight faced by our planet? Hey, Mother Earth can't stay inside, down in the basement, and hide from the sun, like me. She is out there in that relentless sun, day in, day out, and the polar ice caps are sliding into the sea at this very moment, and within one lifetime, my yard, two hundred miles away from the ocean, will be oceanfront property. Let me tell you, there are a lot of reasons why I would never bring a child into this God... wait a minute, Science-forsaken world, and global warming is only one of them. There are a shitton of other reasons, and let me tell you, there are just nights I can't sleep, because I'm up thinking about it all. *That's* why I have insomnia.

So anyway, I'm out there this morning by my shed, with my binoculars, after having been up all night drinking Natty Light, trying to figure out for the life of me how to save this Science-forsaken planet, when the crazy Asian daytrading pimp lunatic neighbor next door steps out the back door and starts pissing again. He was in his customary white bathrobe he never changes out of, just letting that mule meat swing in the wind, piss, piss, piss.

Next thing I see, Captain America comes out and pisses off the side of the porch with him! And I shit you not, the crazy Asian day trading pimp lunatic leans in and kisses Captain America on the cheek! I freaking lowered my binoculars, and just as I did, I saw them turning to face my direction. I put the binoculars back up to my eyes, and both of those guys started shaking their willies at me- and let me tell you, Captain America was as gifted as much as the crazy Asian day trading pimp lunatic- I mean they are *both* packing- and they were laughing, and then they put those things away and they freaking French kissed each other, right there on the back porch, and right for me to see! I mean, I'm not for certain if they knew I was there, because I believe I'm pretty well hidden at that spot, but I think they knew I was there if you know what I mean.

So there's my proof that last night they were indeed having a foursome. And I'm of a mind to think those two faggots were waving their willies at me in the form of an invitation!

Yes, I'm serious!

Anyway, as much as I'd like to stay awake and see if I can get a peek of that hot little Asian whore as she goes to work today, I'm afraid I cannot. I have to go inside and sleep this drunk off. Maybe this evening when she comes home, after I've woken up.

Besides, those two sex freaks are probably going back inside to pull a train on her, and she probably won't be coming out for a long time, anyway. Hey, have you seen some of the stuff on the internet?

Okay, so I've alluded to a few things I know you want explained in detail, so let me bring you up to speed while I nurse this everloving hangover.

No, I didn't get up in time to get a sneak peek of that hot little Asian whore next door as she was coming home. I mean, hell, I may as well call it her house, too, now that she's over there as much as the crazy Asian day trading pimp sex feind lunatic that bought it. But look, I didn't get to go to my spying place and see if I could see her yesterday evening, because I was still so drunk from the night before last that I slept until well after dark, and when I got up, I just sat in front of the bay window with all the lights off and watched the fireflies outside and drank myself to sleep again.

I've been really stressed out lately, with a lot of stuff on my mind. Global warming. Gas prices. I mean, I hardly *go* anywhere, but every time gas prices inch up, tiny little waves of negative effects ripple out across the entire economy. When gas prices go up, shipping prices go up, because what do you think those big rigs run on? Then, of course, the costs of goods and services go up, because the retailers aren't taking the hit. THey're passing it on to us. Hey, I've done the math, over and over, and here's an example. For every ten cents that a gallon of gas goes up, a fifteen pack of Natty Light goes up a nickel. I shit you not. Now, that's not gonna break the bank, but where does it end? When does it stop?

I mean, it's easy to see why a guy like me, who can practically see into the future because of how my brain works, can so easily lose a night of sleep staying up trying to figure this all out. And that Nazi that used to live nextdoor wants to act like there should be nothing less than experience in combat to cause insomnia?

Boy, it's true what they say; ignorance is bliss. I sure wish I wasn't as smart as I am sometimes, so I wouldn't be fully aware of the complete shitstorm mankind is heading for. But alas, I will never enjoy such blissful ignorance, because I was born of gold.

Now, time to move on to that. Being born of certain metals, and how I got my payback on that Nazi nextdoor with my grass. Look, the two go together, because it has to do with birth metals. I'm gold, he was obviously bronze, and he didn't know his place, so I showed it to him. Call me out on stolen valor, will he? Well, in the end, I got him. I got him good!

We'll start with the mailman. Rather, this part time mailman that services this route two or three times a week when my regular mailman, according to this part time guy- this temp scab- calls out sick. It will allow me, in the most simple terms possible, to explain the concept of birth metals so that when I let you know what I did to the Nazi that used to live next door, it will all make perfect sense.

Here's the whole thing about metals. It was a philosophy of Plato's. Yes, that great teacher who had one of the most beautiful minds in the existence of mankind. *He* fully understood the way things should be, and though he's still remembered, by name, and at the household level, sadly, his philosophy on birth metals has been largely forgotten, mostly because most people- sheep, I call them- were born of bronze.

Plato's philosophy was that when men and women are born, they are born into a certain intellectual class. Those born into gold, the class into which I was obviously born, are the leaders. We are at the top, and with our superior intelligence, a true gift of Science, we are to rule the lower classes. Typically, those born of this particular metal, gold, become world leaders, CEO's, that kind of thing. Small business owners, like yacht builders (just saying).

Next, we have those who are born of silver. Though pretty smart people, they're not nearly as smart as those of us who were born of that most precious metal; gold. Now, those born of silver can bear a considerable amount of responsibility, and they make pretty good middle managers, but they could *never* carry out the duties of a world leader or a CEO. Though they make great "right hand man" types, they just couldn't bear the brunt of owning their own business.

And lastly, at the very bottom, we have those who were born of bronze. These are the true slaves of the planet, born to serve those of us who were born of gold, and those who were born of silver. They are meant to be laborers, gophers, lab rat guinea pigs, *and* lower enlisted men in the Army and the Marines. Oh, and temporary mail carriers, filling in for the silver born regular carriers who can call out as much as they bloody well please. Plato's philosophy of birth metals is really not that hard to understand, but so many people at the bronze level just don't get it.

This is how it is all supposed to work. Then, Science-damned capitalism fucked it all up. Prime example; the drunk bastard back in the woods behind me. The man from which we bought the land we built our house on. It's obvious he was born to be a servant; born of bronze. But just because someone somewhere in his family lineage did something a long time ago, he gets to live like he was born of gold, while someone like me, who truly *was* born of gold, the proof of that being that I'm pretty much the smartest person you'll ever meet- I mean, like we've already gone over, I'm so smart I can practically see into the future- has to live a life of bronze, because I'm not greedy, like a Science-damned capitalist, out there seeking wealth.

And then we have unchecked entrepreneurialism! And listen to what I'm saying, the key word here being *unchecked!* I mean, I'm all about working for yourself, because let's face it, a man born of gold, like myself, has *no* business working for anyone born of a lesser metal, hence why I have my own business. I have *tried* working for other people in the past, and they simply are not nearly as smart as me, and it just isn't going to work. *Them* telling *me* what to do? Seriously? It's never lasted more than a week. I've either been fired, because my employer felt inferior in my presence, of I've simply quit, because they were too stupid to even realize how stupid they were compared to me, so I did them the favor of simply leaving.

But hey, back to my point. I cap *my* profit margins, like a *responsible* entrepreneur. I'm not greedy like the capitalists. Entrepreneurialism is about freedom, not wealth! I'm not like that greedy entrepreneurial dirty blonde whore across the way- not to mention the little Asian whore next door- who both worked their way into the silver class after having been born of bronze! Earning money- in a quite nasty fashion, I'll add.

Both of those whores are driving around in new BMW's every quarter! While the vehicle I have- a man born of gold, mind you- is practically being held together with bubble gum and shoe laces! Every day- well, night, as I will *not* go out in that Science-forsaken sun- when I turn the key in the ignition, I pray to the great men of Science that this is *not* the day (well, night) that it refuses to start, because I do *not* have the money to replace it.

Hey, I've been working hard trying to sell this yacht I'm currently working on, but good luck just has *not* been with me as of late. Talk about luck- and that's *exactly* what you need to be successful- boy, I'll *tell* you about luck. Wait until I tell you about the Nazi that used to live over there with the mail order bride, and how they got rich off of the beastealitist's camel!

And the thing that upsets me most about it all is that the man- that Nazi- was born of bronze, and the fact that he was a lower enlisted man in either the Army or the Marines proves it, and yet he's entered the ranks, economically, at least, of the gold by way of his sick neighbor's camel? Yes! And when I tell you that story it is going to make your head explode! I mean, someone is going to be coming into the room you're sitting in right now to clean your brains off the wall!

But first, I need a beer.

...give me a minute...

Ah, Natty Light! Nectar of the Scientists! I don't give a *shit* what that rich kid working down there at the convenience store says!

Okay, let me tell you about that temporary mail carrier. That bronzened born son of a bitch!

So I order most of the small electronic components and various metals (yes, another unapologetic pun) that I need to build my yachts off of the internet, of course, and I have them shipped to my house. UPS and Fedex drops everything off on my front porch, which is perfect, because I can run out and grab the packages if the sun's up and be protected by the shade of the awning of the porch. I'm shaded the whole time I'm out, and the cancer causing rays of the sun can't get me. Well, the USPS is supposed to do the same thing, at least if I order from Amazon Prime and choose parcel select shipping, which is the only method I choose because of this.

Well, let me tell you, that lazy temporary mailman shoves everything that will fit in the mailbox into the mailbox and goes on down the road on his marry ass way, and I have to wait until after dark to walk down to the end of my driveway to get those parcel select packages.

At least, he *used* to.

I put a stop to *that* after he did it a few times. I called the post master and went up one side of that bitch's ass and down the other, and then I wrote a one thousand word long letter, *by hand*, and left it in the box for that bronze born bastard! And he read it, too, because a few days after that, the silver born regular mail carrier came up and knocked on the door and apologized to me for having to put up with that bronze born bastard's incompetence, and he promised me his temp would put all packages on my porch from then on.

Well, the problem was solved, but by Science, I was going to give that temp a piece of my mind the next time I saw him, because I was *right*, and everyone knew it, so I had every right to reiterate that I was right, because I was fucking right!

So, the following week, that bronze born bastard parked down at the end of the drive, turned off his truck, and started coming up the driveway with my package. You see, my driveway is really steep and enters the main road in a sharp turn, and I guess he didn't deem it as safe to back the mail truck out of it into the road, and the pea brained son of a bitch was right about that, at least, because you should *see* how these crazy rich people who live further out the road from me come flying around that turn in their Mercedes Benzes and BMWs. It doesn't help that I don't keep the weeds at the opening of the drive trimmed down, which makes for even poorer visibility, but since I only go out at night anymore, it's okay with me, because if someone's coming around the bend, I can see their headlights. And it's *my* fucking driveway, anyway, not the freaking delivery people's, so what do those weeds have to do with them?

Anyway, here he comes, walking up my driveway, picking mulberries from the mulberry tree limbs overhanging the driveway as he did. What an entitled little ass! I mean, I don't eat them. Not after they sit out in this unfiltered sun the way they do while they're ripening. I buy my fruits and vegetables from Wholefoods, where it's grown, organically, under the ever watchful eyes of organic farmers. There's *no* one out there watching those fucking mulberries grow naturally. Except the deer and the squirrels and the birds, and by Science, that's *exactly* who I let eat them. *I'm* not eating *anything* that grows naturally. There is a *huge* difference between food that grows naturally and food that is grown organically under the ever watchful eyes of organic farmers, and if it's not grown organically by organic farmers it's not going in *my* body.

Anyway, the guy- oh, he's probably in his mid-thirties- he gets up here to the house and I let him have it. "Who do you think you are?" I asked him, and he started muttering on and on about the post office being understaffed, and about how they work you to death, and of how the regular carriers are always calling out sick when they're not, and they can't get fired because they have a union. Well, once he got to that union part, I got *really* pissed! Did he not realize that unions exist to protect the lower working classes, like him, from the greedy fucking capitalists? Well, obviously not, the pea brained bronze born bastard!

At that point, after that union crack, I just let him have it! I told him *exactly* who he is. "You're my temporary mail carrier," I told him. "That's who you are. No more, no less! But if you were to *ever* be anything else, it would be less, because you simply weren't born of the metal precious enough to make you anything more! Do you understand me?" And I got through to him loud and clear, because all he said was, "have a good day, sir," and then he took his happy ass back down the driveway to his shit mail truck and went on his way. Every package that's ever come here by way of USPS since, parcel select or not, has been left on my porch.

Oh, and to deal with his sense of entitlement in regard to those mulberries, I went out there that night- after the sun went down, of course- with a ladder and a pair of limb clippers, and I clipped the lower hanging limbs of those mulberry trees so far up that there's no way he or anyone else can reach the berries now without a six foot ladder. Fucking eat my mulberries! The audacity! It doesn't *matter* that I don't eat them, anyway. The everloving audacity!

Boy, you should have seen him a couple of days later, while he was walking up the driveway, bringing me a package. He was completely shocked when he reached up to grab a mulberry only to find that they were all out of reach. I laughed my ass off while I was down in the basement watching him on one screen by way of the security camera I have out in the drive, and looking to see if I could find my beastealitist neighbor and his camel on the internet on another screen. What a fucking hoot!

Now, let me tell you all about how I put that bronze born *Nazi* bastard that used to live nextdoor, the one married to the mail order bride, in *his* place. I mean I ended up straight out owning that mother fucker, like the slave he was born to be!

Wait a minute...

...oh, my God!

I do *not* believe what I'm seeing! If my eyes are not deceiving me, the little Asian whore next door just came home with that Captain America looking dude again, and the blonde whore's pulling up behind them with *another* dude...

...yep, he's getting out! Let me run out back and grab my binoculars. I'll tell you about how I came to own that bronze born Nazi bastard that used to live nextdoor in a bit. I can't miss this! Oh, this is gonna be rich!

11

What a night they must have had over there last night! Damn, I wish when I was putting cameras up in the driveway over there while the house sat empty that I would have thought to put some inside the house. Boy, if I could have captured what went on over there last night on video? I could have uploaded it to one of those adult sites on the internet and sat back and got paid, Jack!

Okay, so the blonde whore brought some big black buck with her over there last night. I mean, he was a hunk! Looked like that guy in those Rocky spinoff movies, "Creed." Why, with her and him, and the two Asians and Captain America's white ass, they had the whole Science-damn United Nations over there!

And no, that's not a racist joke. As you know, I am tolerant of all races and I am tolerant of interracial relationships. Therefore, that can't even be a marginally off color joke.

Ha! Get it?

Hey, I can get away with making off color jokes about off color jokes, because I'm a... well, you know. And you know I mean nothing by it. It's just funny. I'm merely pointing out the humor with a play on words.

Anyway, same as before. I see all of those dudes kiss, and the girls are kissing each other, and the dudes are kissing the girls, and the girls are kissing the dudes. Hell, I'm just waiting for the beastialitist over on the other side of the hill from them to bring his camel over and get in the mix.

Anyway, let me tell you about how I, a man born of gold, came to rightly own my former neighbor, the Nazi bastard born of bronze.

Basically, I used kindergarten level manipulation techniques, and he was so fucking stupid, he fell for them.

Over, and over and over.

Okay, so here's the deal. It's not that I give a shit about how my property looks. I'm in an affluent area, I mean, we've already determined that all of my neighbors are rich, so I know the value of my land and home is always going to go up. And I don't see the outside of the house. I'm too busy inside the house working for a living, because I wasn't born into affluence like all these crazy rich people around here. So if some of my trees fall and they stay there, decaying on the ground, and the grass gets ass high to an elephant, and it doesn't get cut, it doesn't bother me. What's that got to do with me? And if it bothers any of my neighbors, well let them come and cut my grass and clear up all the fallen limbs and trees. But hey, that's all part of the story.

So, when my bitch ex-wife used to live here, and we had the luxury of having two incomes, as well as all the money her parents always gave her at Christmas (she tried to act like she was the one buying those expensive power tools for my business at Christmas, but I knew it was her parents, gifting her shittons of money each Christmas to lower their net worth in order to avoid the estate tax when they died- remember, we still had that estate tax thing back then) we would hire those Guatemalan guys I've already told you about. The ones I'd set her friends up with to prove her friends were all a bunch of racists. Racists who were no longer welcome in my home.

Anyway, when she left and took that second income with her, I had to make cuts around here in order to keep my yacht business afloat (and no, I'm not sorry for that one, either). So one of the first things that had to go in order to cut costs was lawncare. And no, I was not about to get out there and do it myself, even though one of the last gifts that bitch bought me, rather, one of the last gifts that bitch's *parents* gave her the money to buy me before she left, was a brand new three hundred and fifty dollar Husqvarna weed eater that, to this day, I've never taken out of the box. I do *not* do manual *labor!*

So, I'm outside one day, watching the Nazi lunatic that used to live nextdoor mowing all that grass that wasn't even his. For some reason, the time he'd called me out for not really being a real veteran came to mind, and I felt myself becoming enraged. So the idea of what I would do to him for payback came to me instantly.

I walked over there, all smiles, looking like I actually liked this Science-forsaken world we live in, and I told him how beautiful his yard looked, and I started lamenting about how I didn't really have that much that needed mowed or trimmed, and that part is true, and about how I hated to pay someone to come out here and do it, because the service charge just to come all the way out here from town was more than it would cost to mow it. I told him that it didn't seem big enough for me to even buy lawn equipment, and that I didn't want to pay to have any lawn equipment serviced and maintained.

Man, he took the bait hook, line and sinker! "I'll cut it for you," he says, without even taking a minute to think about it. "I'm out here doing mine anyway. It won't take twenty minutes to do what little you've got. I'll just do it every time I'm out here doing mine."

"Oh, I couldn't let you do that," I said, and I felt like Tom Sawyer suckering that other kid into white washing the fence when I said it.

"Oh, it's no problem, whatsoever. We're neighbors."

"Tell you what," I said, and I am *really* proud of this one. It shows my ability to think on my feet. I mean, this was one of my best manipulative moments of all time. "You guys burn wood in your woodstove in the winter, right?" And just how any good lawyer never asks a question for which he doesn't already know the answer, I already knew the answer. Of *course* they did! They couldn't afford to pay the electric bill in that old shitter house. I think the thing had baseboard heaters.

It's either burn wood and still pay a couple of hundred bucks a month in the winter for electricity or don't burn wood and pay six hundred dollars a month for electricity.

"Yeah, we do," he said.

"Well," I told him, "I had three really big red oak trees fall down in a windstorm last year, just before you guys moved in. If you want to come and cut them up and take the wood to use for firewood, you can have as much of it as you can take for free, since you're willing to mow my grass for free."

"Wow, man! That sounds great!"

"Like you said," I told him. "We're neighbors. What are neighbors for?"

Anyway, I had that pea brained bronze born bastard doing all my outside work! But he's not the only one I manipulated with that deal. You see, when those trees fell, I had an insurance adjuster come out and look at them. I just figured if I could get *any* money out of the deal from the insurance company I'd hire someone to cut the logs up and haul them out- again, not because I cared how it made my yard look- but for the easy money.

Well, the problem was, the insurance company was only willing to give me five grand, because the logs weren't impeding entrance to my home. They were just an eye sore. If they'd fallen on the driveway, I could have gotten three times as much. And you see, the quotes I got for people to come cut the logs and haul them away was well *over* five grand. Everyone wanted three grand per tree, and since this is such an affluent area, all these crazy rich lunatics around here will pay those prices without question, so no one would even budge on their prices. So I was looking at paying nine grand to make five, which would put me four grand in the hole. I'm not stupid.

Enter pea braned, bronze born, dumb hillbilly Nazi lunatic nextdoor!

Cha-ching!

The minute that bastard came over here and started sawing up those logs I was back on the phone with my insurance people. They sent someone out to make sure the work was being done (I'd lied and told them I fronted the worker enough money to get started, but that I needed the insurance payout to pay him the rest), they cut me a check for five grand, and just like that, I had a little bit of money to keep my yacht business going a little longer, at least until I could find someone to buy the yacht I was working on at that time.

So, this went on and on, and I'd test it from time to time, just to make sure I still owned the guy. One time, there was a stick- merely a stick- blocking a little ditch where water would run off of my property and into the ditch line along the state's right of way, and then off from there to the river and then to the sea. Well, the stick was causing the water to come out of the ravine and into the driveway, just a little bit and only after a heavy rain, and I saw that Nazi hillbilly lunatic out there one day, so I went out there and after a minute or so of meaningless smalltalk, I told him I thought I might have to ask the state's department of highways to send some engineers out to fix my backedup ditch. I told him where it was, and he walked over there and not only bent over and removed the stick, which allowed the water to flow freely again, but he took a shovel and dug the ravine out deeper so nothing would get stuck there in the future.

Now listen, I know you're thinking this all sounds manipulative and underhanded and all that, but that guy should have never pressed me on that Navy shit. He brought it all on himself. And besides, it's not *my* fault that I was born of gold and he was born of bronze, making me naturally superior to him. He was born to serve me, not the other way around, so if my man Pluto were still among the living, he'd take my side and grant his full approval of my actions.

However, it did all come to a crushing end one day. The free lawncare and tree removal service. All of it. And I *knew* I was going to risk losing those free services if I were to call the Nazi lunatic bronze born bastard out on his shit, but I took that risk, and I lost my manslave, but it was worth it to let that fucker know *exactly* who he was- a dumb fucking hillbilly, on top of all the other nasty things he was- because he was getting a little too high up on that horse of his, getting rich off of our other neighbor's camel and the biggest bunch of dumb sons of bitches on the internet that you could ever imagine assembling in one place on the internet outside of a Republican political message board. Oh, it's a hell of a story, and the time has come to tell it.

...but wait!

It looks like the orgying members of the United Nations are coming outside to go their separate ways here on this glorious morning after…

...let me go get my optics and watch all of this French kissing that's about to go on between the genders and the races and all that jazz, and then I'll be back to finish my story.

12

I know he's over there laughing at me, that crazy day trading Asian pimp fivesome-sexualistic lunatic! I know it, because I heard him! Him and Captain America and Creed, all of them out there waving their manmeats at me while they were pissing off of the back porch this morning like a bunch of farm animals. You'd think they were all from West Virginia! Hell, maybe Captain America is, for all I know. I know the crazy day trading Asian pimp fivesome-sexualist lunatic isn't. He's from Thailand or something. Creed? I'm sure *he's* not. Hell, those racist, homophobic, white hillbilly Christian bastards over there would probably *lynch* his black ass if *he* even *went* over there.

Which reminds me, speaking of hillbillies. Now, I can't remember exactly *where* that Nazi former Marine, or Army, or whichever military branch he served in that was definitely *not* the Navy or the Airforce that used to live over there was from, but it was *somewhere* in Appalachia. I'm pretty sure it was West Virginia, because that's what put an end to my free lawn care and tree removal. Something I said about West Virginia and Chuck Yaegar. Yeah, the first man to break the sound barrier. We'll get to it. But hey, I *had* to put that bronze born servant in his place, because he and that mail order bride of his got rich off of that beastealitist's camel, and I had to take them down a few notches. They're heads were starting to get too big.

So here's the deal. I can't remember what kind of work those people even did. He might have been a journalist or a blogger or something. It had something to do with writing, I think. Well, anyway, they ended up getting into making YouTube videos. Yes, YouTube videos.

Which reminds me of that prick Byron Blevins! Remember, I told you earlier about that bitch ex-wife of mine always trying to get me to go to game night with her uppity friends? Well, I did, once, just to get her to shut the hell up about it, and that's where I met Byron Blevins and whatever the hell the name of the other guy who was there was. Let me tell you, my gut instinct that night was that those guys and my ex-wife were getting together for threesomes, because that shit is all over the internet, and someone's making that shit, and I'll be damned if my first impression wasn't that my ex-wife and Byron Blevins and whoever the hell that other guy there that night was might be three of those someones.

I mean, Byron Blevins was no looker. He was kind of dorky looking, really, but that other guy? He looked the the definition of a sex fiend. All buff and movie star good-looks, looking. I mean, he was middle aged, like the rest of us, but he sure didn't seem to have *aged* like the rest of us. I'm sure every woman over forty melts like a teenager again just from laying *eyes* on him. He was hot!

So anyway, everything felt wrong about that night. I felt like there was actually some kind of bullshit intervention or something going on. I mean, yeah, I like my Natty Light. It *is* the nectar of the scientists after all, no matter *how* old you are, no matter what that rich bastard cashier thinks, but I have *never* drank a beer because I *needed* a drink. I only drink because I *want* to drink. And these fuckers at game night were trying to pull an intervention on me. I just know it.

I could tell from the very beginning when the first thing they did was offer me a beer. I refused. They were trying to entrap me, and I know it. Sure, they drank and got a little stupid, but I stayed completely sober and kept my wits about me, because I could read this Byron Blevins guy like a book the minute I walked in the door.

You see, Blevins is a counsellor or something. Said it was kind of like a family thing. His father, who's been dead a long time, Blevins was saying, actually used to drive up to D.C. and give weekly counselling sessions to former presidents. He said which ones, but I can't remember. Name dropping son of a bitch. People only do that to make themselves look important.

Anyway, he asked me about my work, and I was explaining about how I build yachts, and he asked me if I could fix stuff. I told him sure, I could fix stuff. I can look at something that's broken, and it's like there's a computer in my head. I don't even need a schematic. I automatically know how to fix it.

"Well," he says, "you know, you could start a YouTube channel and make videos where you show how to fix stuff, and people would watch them when they break something, and in time, believe it or not, you could actually get rich doing it." Like I needed a fucking part-time side job or something away from my yacht building business. I mean, what the hell had my ex-wife been telling him?

I told him I didn't care about being rich, and that I wasn't going to do YouTube. You had to be lucky, anyway, to be one of the people who actually made money at that social media shit. Luck hadn't been going my way as of late, and I didn't think it would change just because I started a freaking YouTube channel.

"Not really," Blevins said, and then he went on and on about his loser little brother. He said the guy, I think his name was Devon, was a writer or something. He said he was good at it, but his heart was in music. He said this Devon kid dropped out of two colleges and was washing dishes downtown at Capture- that's a restaurant and bar on the local downtown mall. Anyway, he said he'd tinker around making cajones- that's a type of percussion instrument, known more commonly as a 'box,' because basically, that's what it is, a wooden box that the percussionist sits on and plays by tapping it- and he met some chick that was a pretty good stock broker, but hated her job, and she was a good singer, and they started a YouTube channel and they went viral and yada, yada, yada, and now they're rich and touring America and they aren't even going to sign a traditional record deal, because they make more money from social media than the music companies are willing to pay them.

"Are you rich?" I asked him. Yes, I just came right out and asked him. And here's why. I do not believe *anything* anyone who is rich says. They can say whatever they want, and people are going to automatically take it as gospel, because they're rich. I learned this long ago.

"I guess so," he said.

"What's that mean?" I asked him. "You either are, or you aren't." Just like the Nazi said to me when he called me out about my Naval service, or in his pea brain, lack thereof. But of course, this whole get together with Byron Blevins et. al. was back before I'd ever met that Nazi and his mail order bride. They hadn't moved in next door to me yet.

Blevins goes on to tell me that when his mom died, his brother, this alleged YouTube sensation, inherited everything, but that he signed it all over to Byron and went on the road with whatever whore of a Florence Nightingale he was shacked up with, and the property was worth millions, as were the stocks, bonds and mutual funds, but he said he still worked- ran his therapy business out of his house- and yada, yada, yada. I knew all I needed to know about Byron Blevons when I found out he was rich. Nothing else he said after that mattered.

And as far as his brother actually being successful on YouTube because he and the whore who sang with him were actually talented goes? Or because they'd worked hard? I'm calling bullshit on that, too. Since the kid was rich, I'm sure he bought his way to the top by way of paying for advertising or something like that. I'm not buying into *any* story *any* crazy rich person tries to sell me.

I'm not stupid!

And whoever that other guy was, I think his name was Steven. One of these assholes out here somewhere is named Steven, it might have been him. But he was just sitting there smirking at me the whole time. I'd look over his way, and every time I did, he was just staring at me, smirking. He was probably thinking about the last time they pulled a train on my wife.

Well, ex-wife, now. Have you seen some of the shit on the internet? Well, I wasn't going to let him have his just jollies. I'd look away from him and that smirk of his just as quick as I'd looked over at them.

Anyway, Blevins kept going on and on about how he'd gotten his start with Region Ten, and then he went to the Veterans Affairs Administration, and then he went into private practice. Let me tell you, I could tell that Byron Blevins was a lunatic, and anyone who ever sat across from him in a counselling session probably left a whole lot worse off than they were before they went. Hell, he said he used to work for the V.A.? I wouldn't be surprised if he didn't counsel that one lunatic veteran that went on that shooting spree over in West Virginia a few years back. I think it was in Beckley. *One* of those little *hick* towns. Shot the whole town up with a deer rifle and then shot himself on top of a bridge and fell into the river below. Can't remember his name. Corey Prine, or something like that. I know they wrote a book about the whole thing, it was such a big deal. The book is called 'Off Switch,' but I've never read it. Hell, I bet that lunatic hillbilly sat across from Byron Blevins at the VA just before that all went down.

Speaking of hillbillies, back to what I was telling you about that Nazi and his mail order bride getting rich off of that sick freak's camel. The guy that lives on the other side of that property over there. Sick bastard and his animal porn. I *know* he's making it.

So, I go over there one day, because I saw the Nazi and his mail order bride outside doing something that seemed a little strange. I asked, of course, *how* they were doing, but my true intentions were to find out *what* they were doing. Turns out, they were making videos to upload on YouTube. They said they were going to give social media a go to see if they could better their financial situation, because I guess he wasn't making much money doing whatever kind of writing he did. I'm sure he wasn't any good at it, I mean, come on, he *was* from West Virginia, and everyone knows those people can't read and write.

Anyway, they were making videos about gardening and tree propagation and all this outdoorsy type shit. Mind you, I'd already met Byron Blevins by this point, and I wanted to show my support. At least make it *look* like I was showing my support. I didn't give a shit, either way, at first, if they succeeded or failed. But I mean, remember, the guy *was* mowing my grass and removing my downed timber for me, so I told him about Byron's brother, and they'd actually heard of the guy. Said someone wrote a book about the whole thing. Called it "The Box" of all things. Said it was on Amazon, but I didn't buy it. I'll *never* buy it. That would be going against everything I believe in. If it were true that Byron's brother was an unchecked entrepreneur, or worse, a capitalist, well, by Science I wasn't supporting him by giving him more money or recognition by buying any damn book written about him.

So anyway, they're over there for months making all these videos and uploading them to YouTube, and frankly, I'd forgotten all about it, until one day I was on YouTube, and son of a bitch, if YouTube wasn't actually recommending one of their videos to me. I mean, I didn't watch it, because I didn't care then, and I don't care now, but I thought that was neat, and it gave me good reason to go back over there and keep my eyes on them. Remember, I'd already sized this guy up as a Nazi. I mean, he was white and middle aged and a veteran of the lower enlisted ranks of either the Army or the Marines, and he was married to a woman of color from a third world country who was young enough to be his daughter. I *had* to keep my eyes on this guy for my own safety. I mean, he lived *right* beside me.

"Would you believe that YouTube actually recommended one of your videos to me?" I said, the next time I saw them outside, which was like, five minutes later, because they were always outside. I tried to warn them about the sun. I told them they were killing themselves with skin cancer being out there in the sun like that all the time, and would you believe they actually laughed at me when I told them that?

Anyway, he says, "YouTube's recommending people around the *world* watch our videos." All high and mighty like. Then his mail order bride said, "we go viral. Five million views one video last month."

Now, she might have barely spoken English, but when she did, it sure did sound nice, and man, she never wore the tight little skirts like that Asian whore over there now does, but she sure as hell wore butt hugging short shorts all the time. Usually some sort of neon pastel color that made her super dark brown skin look even that much more delicious. Hey, I told you. I'm not racist. I don't hate Asians. I'd love to have as much sex with as many of them as I could, and I am honest to Science considering going over there to Southeast Asia and buying me one, just like that Nazi bought her, I'm sure, if I can ever sell the yacht I'm currently working on.

To say I was intrigued is an understatement, because it takes a *lot* to intrigue me. Well, I went back home, and later that day, I watched some of their videos, and you are *not* going to believe this. I mean, when I tell you the story behind their success, and how they would eventually go on to get filthy freaking rich from YouTube, your head is literally going to explode!

You have been forewarned, so proceed with caution.

Okay, so they're plugging along, plugging along, making all these boring videos about planting corn and beans and shit, and all of a sudden, and from out of nowhere, people in the comment section start claiming to see a freaking Bigfoot Sasquatch in the background of the videos. I shit you not. "OMG, what's that large, dark figure just inside the treeline in this video at the twelve minutes and thirteen seconds mark?" people would say. Hell, I guess others would go to the timestamp and look, and sure enough, they were claiming to see it, too, so hell, I would go to the timestamps and look, and you know what it was?

That fucking camel!

That's right. It was that sick bastard's camel that lives on the other side of their property!

Now, you couldn't really see the whole thing, because there's a pretty thick treeline separating the two properties. You could just get a glimpse of it from time to time. You could be watching one of their boring ass videos about stupid boring shit like, how to propogate weeping willow trees from cuttings, and here'd come that fucking two humped camel named Sally, on the other side of the property line. She'd start eating the leaves off of a tree or something, and the damn next thing you know, everyone's commenting that Bigfoot Sasquatch is back there in the woods, pulling the branches down so he or she, or hell, it, could see what this Nazi and his mail order bride were doing.

Hell, sometimes, they'd say *they*, because if Sally were to pass through where there happened to be a break in the foliage along the treeline on the properties' border, and they got a quick glimpse at *both* of her humps, they'd claim there were *two* Bigfoot Sasquatches back in the woods. There were even times when that damn camel's entire head was sticking through the treeline, and it's face was staring right into the camera, and the mother fuckers who watched this guy's YouTube channel would proclaim it was the head and face of Bigfoot Sasquatch!

Now, I have to hand it to the bronze born Nazi hillbilly bastard. He saw what was going on, and he picked up the stick and ran with it! I mean, he started milking that shit for all it was worth, and I guess it was worth a *lot*! They went from driving some beat up piece of shit S.U.V. they had, I mean, the back hatch wouldn't even open- and I remember him specifically telling me they didn't have the money to get it fixed- to driving a brand new four wheel drive pickup truck that *had* to cost sixty grand! They started buying mountain bikes and kayaks, and, well, I thought more, but I was wrong. Trust me, there's more to the story, and if your head hasn't exploded yet, it will once I tell you the rest.

So when I saw what was going on, I went over there one day to ask them how they were doing. Of course, I really just wanted to know *what* they were doing and *how* they were doing it. So after a minute's worth of meaningless small talk, I said, "Man, can you believe how stupid those people who watch your videos are?" They both looked at me with this stupid blank look on their faces. "Huh?" they said, like they didn't know what I was getting at.

"Come on," I said. "Bigfoot? Sasquatch? People actually *believe* that shit? And you guys are making a *fortune* off of that shit?"

Well, I guess he didn't like me speaking the truth. Those fucking conservatives. They hate facts. I fact check anything any damn one of them says to me, which isn't much, because I avoid them. I can tolerate almost anything, because I am a tolerant liberal, but I can*not* tolerate conservatives.

"We just kind of view it as if the people who watch our videos are being entertained," he said. "I mean, sure, some of them are seeing some things in the woods. But some of them just like our gardening videos, or whatever."

"Some of them just like us," the little mail order bride said. Yeah, I bet some of them just like looking at her and fantasizing about all you can eat Chinese, if you know what I mean. No, she wasn't Chinese, but you know what I mean. And there's nothing racist about that, because…

…do we really need to go over this again?

So, over time, I sat back and watched them get rich off of that bullshit. They'd go out there in the woods, acting all scared and shit, like they were looking for Bigfoot Sasquatch. And I could see exactly what they were doing from here. Well, from out there beside the woodshed with my binoculars. Now, he hadn't put those trees up by that time- the leyland cypress trees I told you about- so I had a better view of the whole place back then. I'd watch them map out their strategy. They'd wait for Sally to get within view from their place, hell, sometimes they'd feed her treets to get her to where they wanted her, then they'd walk a couple hundred yards away from her and start making their video and just talk about whatever mumbo-jumbo they were talking about- I never listened to it when I'd watch their videos (I just read the damn comments to make fun of all the stupid people), and once they got up to where that camel was, they'd act like they'd found Bigfoot Sasquatch and they'd run off like they were scared as shit, and that would be the end of the video.

And people were watching by the millions!

Hell, I remember the time I noticed they weren't home for a week, which was odd, because they'd never gone anywhere even for a single night the whole time they'd lived there up until that point. Sure, I went over and peeked into all the ground level windows to try to figure out what was going on. All their stuff was still in there, so I knew they'd be back. It was summer, so I figured since they were actually making all that money they probably just went on vacation, so of course that got me curious as to where they went.

The day they came back, I was over there and on them before they even had time to close their truck doors after getting out of the vehicle.

"Oh, my God! Are you guys okay? Where have you been?" I said. Of course I didn't give a shit about how they were doing, if they were okay or not. I just wanted to know *what* they'd been doing.

"We go beach," the woman said. Man, she was already dark, but after a week in the sun she was way darker. She looked black now instead of brown.

"We went to the Outer Banks," the Nazi said. "It's been years since we took a vacation, so we thought we'd take one."

"I was worrying so much about you guys you'd think I was Jewish," I told him. I was trying to get him to laugh at that to prove that he's antisemetic, but he didn't take the bait. I thought maybe he hadn't heard me, so I said it gain. "I was worried so much about you guys you'd think I was Jewish. People tell me I must be Jewish as much as I worry. I tell them I wish. I'd have more money." I just laughed and laughed, fake laughs, of course, because as a progressive liberal I certainly do *not* tolerate anti-semitism. I only made those anti-semitic sounding comments to set this Nazi up. Again, keyword here, anti-semetic *sounding*. Since I'm a progressive liberal, it simply isn't possible for me to be anti-semetic, so I can pretty much say what I want about Jews. It can*not* be taken seriously.

Anyway, he never took the bait on that one at all, so I dropped it and I told them I hoped they had a good time, which they said they did, and then I left.

But you know what *really* got my goat about their YouTube channel? Their viewers were in on the joke! They *had* to be! Either that or they really thought the shit was real. These people were timestamping where they were seeing Bigfoot Sasquatch, and saying they were just as scared watching the video as the Nazi and his little mail order bride must have been when they were making it.

Hell, I would go onto their YouTube channel, under fake profiles, of course, and try to help these people. Those viewers who either thought that shit was real or who were in on the joke. I would tell them how stupid they were for believing these fake videos. I would tell them that Bigfoot wasn't real, and they were all a bunch of idiots, and they were being fooled by a charlatan. Hell, everytime I did that, though, that bronze born Nazi hillbilly bastard would block my user profile. I bet I made more than two dozen different fake accounts to troll that son of a bitch and that little mail order bride whore of his, and Science-damn if they didn't block them all!

But you know what? Before he banned each of my fake profiles because of the comments I left, my comments would stay up for a couple of hours before he got around to seeing them, and would you believe his viewers would actually bust my chops in the replies?

No shit!

Here I was, trying to help them by letting them know that none of this nonsense was real, and they would reply to my comments and tell me that I didn't have to watch the videos. They would tell me to go watch another channel. I mean, I couldn't get through to these people. They were like a freaking cult!

Anyway, I'd finally had it. I mean, these fans of theirs, I found out from talking to him one time, were actually *buying* them most of the expensive shit I thought they were buying for themselves from their YouTube earnings. I mean, I saw him come home one day hauling a brand new gasoline powered log splitter behind his brand new pickup truck, so I went over to ask him how they were doing, but of course, I really just wanted to know *what* they were doing, and I found out one of their viewers actually bought them that log splitter. Seriously! And the thing must have cost fifteen hundred dollars!

"You'd better not leave her out here alone," I said, making my way over through their yard. "I hear there's a Bigfoot Sasquatch around here somewhere. He might see her out here and decide he wants to eat Chinese."

"Um, she's not Chinese," he said, and he looked confused.

"Yeah, but you *get* it, right? Bigfoot might decide he wants to eat Chinese if he sees her out here alone, *get* it?"

"Actually, I don't," he said. "She's not Chinese," he said again, like he hadn't heard me the first two times.

Look, to be honest about it, I was testing him, just like I had been before with the Jewish jokes. I *knew* he was a racist Nazi. He fit the profile. I mean, he was a post middle aged white man from West Virginia. And a veteran of the lower enlisted ranks of either the Army or the Marines, *not* the Navy or the Air Force. How could he *not* be a racist Nazi? I was trying to get him laughing about my joke, which I'll admit was a bit racist, but only because I wanted him to fall into my trap so I would have undeniable evidence that *he* was a racist Nazi. I mean, that's how manipulation works. You act like you're of the same mindset. On the same side, so to say. Like good cop in good cop bad cop. But he would *not* take the bait. Nope. He just said, "are you sure what you're saying is really appropriate?"

"Look," I said, and I'll say it again here. "I can't be racist. I'm a progressive liberal."

You know what that son of a bitch said next? He says, "I don't think you're quite as progressive as you think you are."

I know, right? A fucking bronze born racist Nazi hillbilly saying that to me? A man born of the metal of gold who not only is *not* from Appalachia, but who has never stepped foot in Appalachia? I'm not going over there around those people! Everyone knows *exactly* what they're like, and it's why I've never been over there in the first place! A progressive minded individual like myself wouldn't be *safe* over there. I'm sure they'd lynch me as quickly as they'd lynch any gay, black, or *transgeder* person!

Well, that did it. He took my attempt at entrapment as if *I* was the racist, so I decided I was going to put him in his place once and for all, and I sure did show *him*. Like I've already told you, it cost me my free lawn care and tree removal service, but I showed him his place, so it was all worth it.

First, I wanted to make it look like I wasn't upset that he'd pretty much insinuated that *I* was the racist, because of what I'd said about Bigfoot wanting to eat Chinese. So I kept going with the small talk. I asked him just how much money they were making on YouTube, anyway. When he told me, it became extremely difficult to maintain my composure. Those two were making far more money in one month from those stupid, fake Bigfoot Sasquatch videos than I make in an entire year making and selling my handmade custom yachts!

To be honest about it now, I was *pissed*, and boy, did I instantly hate them even more than I already did, but still, I was going to put them in their bronze born places once and for all and be done with them, so I didn't let my anger show. Hey, I already told you that I hate rich people, and they'd obviously joined their ranks, so they were now on my hate list at the highest level. A couple of unchecked entrepreneurs is what they were. Greedy as any fucking capitalist that ever existed, making money like that. It was time for me to wash my hands of such scum.

"You're familiar with West Virginia, aren't you?" I said.

"Yeah?" he said. But he said it like a question. Like he was trying to figure out what I was getting at. I always got the impression this guy was trying to figure out what I was up to. Like he didn't trust me. Almost like someone had warned him about me for some reason. Well, I sure didn't trust him, either.

"I'm sure you know of Chuck Yeager then, don't you?" I said, and this was all back before Yeager died, of course.

"Of course," he said, and he lit up like a fucking Christmas tree. I knew he would. Chuck Yeager is like a Scientist to those dumb hillbillies. He's like, the only one of them to do something with his life. Well, and Don Knotts, if you would consider being Barney fucking Fife doing something with your life.

"I met him once," I told him.

Now, mind you, this wasn't even true. But like *that* matters. I was going to crush this racist hillbilly Nazi once and for all, and name dropping is always a good setup. You know, it really *does* make you look important if you tell people you know someone who's important. It's arrogant, sure, and that's another thing I didn't like about that Byron Blevins guy, name dropping the presidents his father used to counsel. Like I'm supposed to automatically grant him more respect because of who his father knew? Well, most people will grant respect to name droppers, but I'm not most people. I'm way smarter than most people, so *I'm* the one to drop the names, whether I've met the people whose names I drop or not. This isn't about honesty. This is about gaining control through manipulation. One must do what one must do. And when you drop the name of their idol? And then you crush their idol? Oh, you get to watch them melt!

"How did you meet Chuck Yaeger?" he asked. He was taking the bait hook, line and sinker. He always did, the dumb hillbilly Nazi.

"When I was in R.O.T.C. in college," I said. I would have told him when I was in the Navy, but he'd already figured that one out when he decided to press me on basic training. "He came to speak to us about leadership."

"That must have been a pretty awesome experience," he said. And he was still glowing like a Christmas tree on Christmas morning.

"Not really," I said, and I used my best 'play it down' tone.

"How could meeting a living legend like Chuck Yaeger not be awesome?" he said.

"Because it doesn't matter what Chuck Yaeger has done," I said. "He'll never be anything more than a dumb fucking hillbilly from West Virginia."

Boy, after I said that, that misogynistic racist hillbilly bronze born Nazi bastard didn't say a word. It was like I just stuck a stake right through his heart. I turned and walked off and I never went back.

Oh, he stopped mowing my grass after that, and he never came back over and cleared any of my fallen timber. But I didn't care. Like I said, I'm not the one that sees the outside of my house. I'm too busy staying inside working. Not all of us are lucky enough to be rich simply from having been born into the right family, like most of these crazy rich people around here, or lucky enough to be able to find a bunch of like-minded dumb hillbillies who will watch videos with a camel in the woods and swear up and down it's a damn Bigfoot Sasquatch, and get rich that way. Some of us have to actually work.

But I'd made my point.

I put him back in his place.

He understood I was born of gold.

And he was born of bronze.

13

Well, there hasn't really been anything out of the norm to report on what's been going on with the day trading sex addicted crazy Asian pimp lunatic nextdoor as of late. Sure, his little whore friend, the Asian one, still comes and goes daily, and boy, does she ever *still* look good. The blonde bimbo from across the way comes and goes as much as she ever did. Captain America is still pretty regular, but Creed only comes by every now and then. It's like their big honeymoon period wore off at some point this past blistering hot summer. Hell, I don't know, maybe that lunatic's labido is starting to drop. But now that it's fall, things are a lot quieter than they were back in the spring, when that lunatic over there had just moved in and all the excitement of newness was still new. Yeah, that's redundant, but so are most people, so what.

I was out here watching over there, through my binoculars, of course, until an hour or so after dark tonight, wondering if they'd get any trick or treaters. It's Halloween night and all, but we live so far out of town no one comes trick or treating out here. My ex used to have a few kids come out with their parents, you know, since she taught school and all- she'd invite her favorites- and what a drag *that* was. I had to act like I gave a shit. Put on my best "Mr. Teacher's Spouse" face and act like I liked their costumes or whatever. Would you believe she actually printed up a tee shirt that said "Teacher's Spouse" on it and made me wear it when she'd rope me into going to those stupid teachers functions they were always having down at the school? What an embarrassment *that* was. I mean, why didn't *she* just wear a shirt that said, "I'm carrying my husband's balls around in a jar inside my purse?" But I wore it, to keep the peace.

I've been lying here on the top of the hull of the yacht I'm currently working on, looking up at the stars. Today was just one of those bright, clear, beautiful fall days that makes everything feel nostalgic, so I wheeled the hull out of the storage shed and into the light, something I haven't done in forever, because it's not like I'm trying to intentionally get skin cancer or something, but I wanted to see her in her full glory. I found some rust on some of the fittings from where it's been damper than I would prefer, I guess, inside the shed where I keep her. I'll have to go back over each and every one of them again to get the rust off, but oh well. I mean, sure, this is how I make my money, but I'll admit, it's also a labor of love. I tell ya, if I had a nickel just for the number of times I've gone around taking rust off of fittings I've already assembled, I wouldn't ever even *need* to *sell* a yacht.

Lying here tonight, looking up at the stars, I can't help but be taken back to the time when I fell in love with boats, the water, hell, love in general. It's been forty years ago now, but at times like this, when the stars are aligned right, and the night is clear and crisp, it all comes back to me, as if it were only yesterday.

I had a best friend once. His name was Lenny. Lenny's family had a Bayliner, and they spent most of the summer on it up at Lake Anna. Lenny always asked me to go along, and you'd better Science-damn well *believe* I went along.

Lenny and I had been best friends since kindergarten. His father was a retired Naval officer, and he never lost his love for the water even after retirement. The thing I remember most about when they moved in when they bought the house down the street from ours was seeing that big Bayliner attached to the back of their truck when they showed up. I walked out of our house, in awe, right down the street to their house, and I never took my eyes off of that boat.

"Want to take it out for a spin sometime, kid?" I heard a voice say. I turned around, and Lenny's dad was standing behind me, smiling as I admired his boat. His name was Leonard, but we all called him Admiral. He told us to call him Leonard, but there was something majestic about calling him Admiral, so that's what we called him, even though he always insisted we call him Leonard. Yep, if I had to go back and mark the time in my life when I knew without knowing that I was going to grow up and be a boat builder, that was the time.

Now, you're probably wondering why I chose yachts instead of Bayliners. Well, that's because that's what I told Lenny I would do. For us. Me and him. The best friend I ever had.

The years would pass and Lenny and I would become soulmates. Sure, it felt like we were brothers after knowing each other for just a short while, but once we got up into our teenage years, it became something far more than that. Something that didn't even resemble brotherhood. It was simply too strong.

When we were sixteen, the Admiral would let us take the boat out alone. Just me and Lenny. Now you talk about *fun*. We did everything two sixteen year old boys would do with a boat and freedom, which pretty much translates to everything you're not supposed to do. We'd make giant waves in the no wake zone. We'd see people fishing along the lake bank and we'd wave-blast them. That's what we called it. It might be called something else, when you go as fast as you can and then cut a sharp turn angled at the bank to blast it with a wave, but that's what we called it. Wave-blasting!

But my favorite was when we'd go camping on the boat. Not *with* the boat, but *on* it. We'd take a tent and everything, and we'd tell the Admiral that we were mooring on the shore at night and camping on land, but it was all a lie. We'd ride out into the very middle of the lake and then we'd just kill the engine. We'd always wake up on a different part of the lake the next morning. It might not have been the safest thing to do, but it was the most enjoyable way to do it, camping that is, as far as *we* were concerned.

I remember that summer when we were sixteen. I remember that night- clear like this very Halloween night, not a cloud in the sky and the stars shining brightly- but it was much warmer, of course. There might have been high humidity on land, but not out on the water. There was a light breeze and it was blowing any humidity that might have been away.

"I could do this forever," Lenny said. He was lying on his side facing me. I was lying on my side facing him. We had our sleeping bags rolled out in the middle of the hull, but we weren't *in* them, we were *on* them. It was far too warm to be inside them. We were lying there, in only our underwear, each holding our heads propped up, facing the other, enjoying the moment.

"Let's do it, then," I said. "Forever. Just me and you."

"We'll need a boat," Lenny said. "But a Bayliner isn't good enough. We need something bigger."

"We need a *yacht*," I said.

"A yacht!" he said, shocked. "Do you know how expensive those things are? How in the *hell* are we going to be able to afford a yacht?"

"I'll build us one," I said, without even thinking. The words just came out.

"You're crazy," Lenny said, and he threw his head back in laughter. He settled down and then he went back to facing me and he said, "you know, though. I've seen some of your work from shop class. You're pretty good. Maybe you *could* build us a yacht?"

"If I build us a yacht," I said, "would you live on it with me? Just us? So we really *could* do this all the time?"

"I would live anywhere with you, just us, so we could really do anything we wanted all the time," he said. "Boat or not."

At that moment, it occurred to me just how beautiful his eyes were. They were blue, and I could see a million stars reflected in them, from the way he held his head in his palm, facing me.

I noticed how perfect his skin was. I struggled with acne off and on, but Lenny never had a zit in his life. And his lips were rosy, as if they were always a little bit warm, and though it was summer, I could think back on past winters and remember that his lips looked just as warm and inviting during the coldest times of the year as well.

I edged forward, just a bit, because we were already so close, and I kissed him, and

Bam!

He punched me right in the face, and he said, "I'm not fucking gay!" And he jumped to his feet and automatically assumed a boxer's stance. "I am not fucking!" he screamed again.

I stood up, my lip bleeding, and I told him I was sorry. "I know you're not gay," I said. "I'm sorry. I'll never do it again, Lenny, I promise."

"I'm a fucking boy! I'm not a fucking girl! I have a penis, goddamn it!" he shouted next, and he pulled his right fist back like he was going to hit me again. I covered up and I told him, "I know, Lenny. I know you're not a girl. You're not a girl and you're not gay. I'm sorry. I'll never do it again."

He relaxed. He let down his arms, but only a dumbass would forget that that's exactly how the great Ali used to lure people in for the knockout punch, so I didn't get any closer.

"So you know I'm not gay," Lenny said, and I could tell by the tone of his voice he was beginning to calm down.

"Yes, Lenny. I know you're not gay. I don't see you that way."

"And I'm not a girl?" he said, but it sounded more like a question. And it seemed more like he was questioning himself, not me. "I have a penis. I *can't* be a girl." And it really seemed like he was having a conversation with himself, not me. It almost felt like I wasn't even there, but my throbbing and bleeding lip let me know I very much was there.

"No, Lenny," I said. "I don't think that at all. That's not how I see you. Neither of those things."

"Then how do you see me?" Lenny asked, and he looked at me, making eye contact with me for the first time since he'd hit me.

"As you," I said.

"And who *am* I?" he said, again sounding more like he was questioning himself, not me.

"The most beautiful person in the world," I said.

He stepped toward me, and I didn't feel threatened. It's hard to describe what I felt. I would say *real*, if that makes any sense, because I'm not sure if I even know what real *is* anymore. I've had two wives in my lifetime, and I've made love to both of them, and I enjoyed making love to both of them, but I never felt anything *nearly* as close with either of them as what I felt that night with Lenny on that boat, under the stars, the summer we both turned sixteen.

Once Lenny had closed the distance between us, he leaned in to kiss me. I reciprocated. We kissed, the only *real* kiss, to this day, that I think I've ever had. And then…

Bam!

He punched me again, and this time he got me in the nose, and I could feel *and* hear it break.

"Don't you *ever* fucking kiss me again, you goddamn faggot!" he yelled at me. "And if you *ever* tell *anyone* about this, I will bring you out here and I will fucking drown you! Do you understand me?"

"Yes, Lenny," I said. I'd made my way over to the side of the boat and I was leaning slightly over the side so the blood pouring out of my nose would go into the water. I was crying like a baby, but it wasn't so much because my nose was broken, or so much because it hurt, because it hurt like a mother fucker, but because I was *heart* broken. That's the night my heart was broken and it hasn't healed since.

Neither of us slept that night. At least I know *I* didn't. We sat at opposite ends of the hull, curled up within ourselves, even though it wasn't cold.

The next morning we talked things over. Lenny started the conversation by apologizing for beating the shit out of me. He said he felt terrible about it. I asked him if it hurt him more than it hurt me, and we had a real, genuine laugh about that, and we opened up, but only so much with each other, and we had a gentleman's agreement that we'd never tell anyone about what happened the night before, and that we would never have any sort of physical contact with each other like that again. We made up some bullshit story about how we were joyriding in the boat after dark, and that I was standing up too high when we got too close to the bank and a tree limb caught me in the face. Everyone bought it.

About six months later, I got a phone call from the Admiral. He was crying and he asked me if I could come over and hug Lenny's mom; calm her down. "What's wrong?" I asked. "Lenny's dead," he told me. They'd found him hanging by his belt in his closet. Lenny's mom was hysterical, and the Admiral needed help calming her down. He told me an ambulance was on the way, though he knew they needed a hearse instead, but he was wondering if I could come over. I went, and though their house was only fifty yards down the street from ours, that day, it seemed like I was taking the longest walk I'd ever taken in my life.

There was a funeral at the end of the week, and no one could figure out why Lenny had taken his life. The Admiral kept questioning me, like I had the answer. Sadly, I believe I *did* have the answer, but as Lenny's best friend, I was going to take that answer to the grave with me. Just like Lenny did.

Besides, those were different times, and the Admiral was a hard man. He'd served his country and fought in Vietnam, back during the early "advisor" days, when most Americans had still never heard of the place. I wasn't about to inform him that not only did he lose his son at sixteen years young, but that his son was, well, whatever he was.

Lenny was *not* gay. I was *not* attracted to him because of his gender. I've never been attracted to another man in my life. I mean, I don't *think* I have been. Can anyone ever truly be sure? Either way, it had nothing to do with *what* Lenny was, but it had everything to do with *who* Lenny was. And I never felt for either of my wives what I felt for Lenny. I don't believe gender has anything to do with it. All I know is that Lenny was beautiful, and I loved him.

My father pulled me off to the side as everyone was funnelling out of the funeral services. My dad wasn't a vet, but he was a hard ass. Worked construction his whole life. A man's man. He'd worked his way up into crew leader and then eventually owned his own construction company. Two things I remember he loved most when I was growing up; Ronald Reagan and whoever was playing against the Dallas Cowboys on Sundays.

"I'd better *never* find out anything was going on between you and Lenny," he told me, looking around all paranoid like, making sure no one was watching. I could always tell my father never liked Lenny, but I never knew why. He was the nicest kid in school. Never got into any trouble. Everyone liked him. Well, everyone except my dad.

"Like what?" I asked.

"You know *exactly* what I mean," my father said, and his eyes drilled into mine, and he said, "if a man's a queer, that's his business, and that's his right. But when it comes to my son?" he paused, looking around, again making sure no one was watching, and then his eyes drilled into mine once again, and he said, "well, let's just say I'd rather my son be *dead* than be *queer*."

I never told anyone about Lenny and me and that night on the boat. My father's dead now, as is the Admiral, so neither of them ever knew about us, but I really do believe that they both knew about us. I know that sounds like an oxymoron, but only because it is, and you know what I mean by it. Just because some things are never spoken does not mean that those things are never known.

What the fuck…

…damn, it looks like the Asian whore and the blonde bimbo are out in the backyard building a *fire*. They're screaming something. I can't really hear them very well. I'm going to have to get closer…

…let me grab my binoculars…

14

…well, I'll be Science-damned!

They're having, like, some sort of old fashioned Samhain festival or something over there. They've got a bonfire going and everything. They're dancing around it, just the two of them in those little microskirts they both like wearing so much. Captain America and Creed are nowhere, and surprise, surprise, I'm not seeing the lunatic.

Hey, I wonder why he's not out there with them?

You know what? The fuck with it all. I've holed myself up long enough. I might not think too highly of those whores over there, but they don't mind being themselves and showing the world who they are, at least not the *neighbors*, so I'm going to go right over there and join them!

Wait a minute…

…what was that?

They're screaming the lunatic's name! Like they're calling him out!

Holy shit! They're screaming they hate him! I'd better not go over there just yet! I'd better hunker down right here behind this old oak stump right here on the property line- this is close enough to them for now- and keep my eyes on this shit. Looks like we might be having us a good old fashioned domestic dispute next door!

Holy shit! They're screaming that they're going to kill him! 'Tonight's the night you die!' they're saying. 'Tonight's the night you die!' They're screaming it over and over!

Holy Mary, mother of Science, they're going into the house…

...I'm getting closer...

...holy shit! They're throwing shit around inside the house! I can hear stuff banging around against the walls, slamming on the floor...

...I just heard a loud thump and a grunt! Mother fucker! I think they just *killed* the son of a bitch!

They're coming back out. Oh, shit! I gotta hide! I'm right here in the fucking yard!

Just don't move. It's dark. They can't see me. Just don't move.

Holy shit, they're throwing all of his clothes in the fire. 'He's dead!' they're saying to each other, over and over. 'He's dead! That man will *never* see another sunrise!'

Oh, my Science! They're hugging and kissing and telling each other they *love* each other!

Science damn! This is just like that one movie, "Wild Things" with that totally awesome twist at the end, where it turns out those two little teenaged sociopaths were lesbian lovers. This has been their damn ruse over here with my lunatic neighbor all along! They were using that Crazy Asian day trading pimp lunatic son of a bitch for his money, and once they got it all, which they obviously *have*, they fucking killed him!

Holy shit!

...wait...

...they're done hugging and kissing. Blondey is leaving. She's walking down the driveway to go home. I heard her tell the Asian whore she'll see her tomorrow...

...once that blonde bimbo crosses the road, I'm sneaking out of here...

...there she goes...

I'm fucking out of here!

Running... running... running!

"Hey, you!"

Oh, shit, she's coming! The Asian whore! She's fucking chasing me!

"You sick fucker! I've had enough of your prying eyes!"

Oh shit! Oh, shit! Oh, shit!

Gotta make it to the house!

Gotta get my gun!

Oh, fuck, the steps...

...front porch...

...door.

Oh, fuck!

Gun...

"Hey!"

Stop right there or I'll shoot! I know exactly who you are, and I know exactly what's going on! I'll fucking shoot you!

"Wow! You'd actually fucking shoot me because..."

BANG!

Phone... phone.

Gotta find my phone.

Call 911. This was self defense. I can't get in trouble. That bitch killed the fucking lunatic nextdoor, and I was next, because she knew I saw.

Self defense.

Ah, shit.

Here's my phone.

Dialing...

...911...

"911, what's your emergency?"

The Next Day

*From The Daily Exponent

'Murder Suicide Hate Crime Shocks Small Farming Community'

"A murder suicide hate crime has shocked a small farming community outside of Charlottesville, Virginia. Last night, on Halloween Night, a fifty six year old white male, Timothy Gardener, a convicted felon in the illegal possession of a firearm, shot and killed a twenty eight year old transgender woman of Puerto Rican descent before committing suicide by shooting himself with the same illegally possessed firearm. Authorities have said the weapon used for the murder suicide hate crime was a .38 caliber handgun which had not been obtained though legal means. Authorities are still trying to determine how a convicted felon obtained such a weapon, but their efforts have so far been futile, as the weapon, obviously, is not registered.

"'There is a reason felons are not allowed to own firearms,' Virginia Commonwealth's Attorney, Julian Rodriquez, Democrat, told reporters at a news conference the morning after the murder suicide hate crime. 'As you know, I am up for re-election this fall, and you'd better *believe*, after this tragedy, I am going to push for even *more* gun control and even stronger gun law violation penalties. This senseless act of hate would have never been carried out if it weren't so simple for anyone, including convicted felons, to obtain firearms.'

"'Somebody should have seen this coming,' fifty five year old Susan Riley, one of thousands of protestors in front of Charlottesville City Hall told reporters after the news conference. 'I mean, a single, middle aged, conservative white man living out there in the woods by himself? How does that *not* perfectly fit the profile of a homophobic, transgenderphobic, xeonophobic nutcase? And for a guy like that- a *Republican*, no doubt- to have guns? Even after a felony conviction? I mean, I heard the guy had a whole *arsenal*. As tragic as last night's hate crime was, we're just lucky he didn't walk into a school and blow away a bunch of kids.'

"'The guy was a total lunatic,' Bobby Jenkins, a local man who works at a small convenience store just outside of Charlottesville, told reporters. 'Yeah, I knew him. Guy totally gave me the creeps. He only came in at night, to buy beer, but even though it was dark, he always had sunscreen caked all over his skin.

"'I tried to make small talk with him once,' Jenkins told reporters. 'I don't know. I said something about the brand of beer he was buying, and dude totally went *off* on me. Started screaming about hating rich people, or something. I was like, 'hey man, I feel ya. I'm not rich. I'm working here while my wife finishes up her nursing degree, then she's gonna work and I'm gonna go to college. We have a kid man, so we gotta take turns going to school and working and stuff. I'm with ya.'

"'I was trying to make him feel connected, you know, and I was being honest,' Jenkins added. 'I mean, if I were rich, do you think I'd be pulling graveyard shifts at the convenience store? I wish I had called the cops on the guy back then. I mean, it was easy to see he was one of those right-wing conspiracy nut jobs. I should have known it was just a matter of time before he'd blow away some poor immigrant or someone who was black or gay, or something. I bet he's really proud of himself, down there in hell, having murdered someone who was so many of the things he hated.'

"'I *knew* they let him off easy,' Sarah Bohner, the murderer's first wife told reporters when reached by telephone at home. When called, she had not yet heard the news. 'They gave him six months unsupervised probation on a plea bargain. It wasn't enough, and I *knew* something like this would happen someday. Damn, I wish they would have given him a harsher sentence.'

"Nearly twenty years prior to last night's heinous hate crime, Gardener entered a felony plea agreement on a charge of bank fraud. 'He'd asked me to co-sign a business loan application for him six months after we were married,' Bohner told reporters. 'I refused to do it. I'd already figured out he was the kind of guy who never finished anything he started, so I wasn't going to risk my credit. He got so angry, he pushed me into a wall. I should have left him then and there, but I was dumb enough to stay.

"'Less than a month later,' Bohner continued, 'I noticed he'd somehow come into a pile of cash. He told me the bank had given him approval without me co-signing the loan application after all. He apologized again for having, 'lain hands on me,' that's how he worded it, but my gut was telling me something wasn't right. Sure enough, when I checked my credit report, I saw that there was a fifty thousand dollar business loan in my name showing up on my Experian credit report. When I told him I was leaving him, and that I was going to report him, he pushed me again. I fell to the floor, and when I saw the look in his eyes, I was terrified. I've never been that scared in my life. The man, I could tell, was a lunatic, and I ran for my life!'

"According to court records, Gardener had not only forged his former wife's signature on loan applications, but he had claimed property that was not his, a storage shed where he kept the partially built hull of a boat he was building, as his own, and used the property as collateral to secure the bank loan. Gardener was facing twenty years in prison for bank fraud, but he took the plea agreement, forever giving up his voting rights and his rights to own firearms, in exchange for not having to go to prison. He did six months of unsupervised probation.

"'Talk about a lunatic,' Joey Campbell of the Campbell soup family dynasty told reporters. 'This man was the definition of the word.'

"Campbell, though wealthy, works as a temporary mail carrier in Albemarle County, and he serviced Gardener's route on occasion when Gardener's regular mail carrier was off. 'The regular carrier on that route warned me about the guy,' Campbell told reporters. 'But I had no *idea* it was true. What he told me about him. Like, the guy was a vampire or something. Never came out during the day, and I had to leave his packages on his porch.

"'Well, I put one in the mailbox once, and this dude totally lost his crap. Wrote some kind of letter I never wasted my time reading, and then came out and yelled at me and called me a peasant, or something.'

"When asked if he informed Gardener that he was actually wealthy, and that he, like most of his family members, still worked, despite their wealth, because they feel compelled to contribute to society, Campbell said, 'no. That lunatic wasn't worth my time. He just struck me as some kind of crazy redneck right winger who thinks vaccines are the mark of the beast, or something. The kind of guy that buys into religion over science, you know. I was already behind on my route that day, so I just kept moving on.'

"'Trust me, he was a cold hearted son of a (explicit) who hated everyone," David Jones, a neighbor of Gardener's, told reporters. "He didn't just kill that woman because she was transgender or Puerto Rican. He would have killed her for no reason at all if he'd had the chance. I mean, the man hated everyone!'

"'Let me tell you,' Jones said, going further into detail. 'He just stood there, and through those binoculars he was always using to commit voyeurism on everyone, watched as my nephew damn near died of a heart attack. I mean, he could have done anything to help, call 911 or something, but he did absolutely nothing!'

"Jones claims that his nephew, Steven Jones, who lived in a house across the road from Gardener, moved to the area just before Gardener moved to the area himself. An antique enthusiast, the younger Jones specialises in rebuilding antique tractor motors. He and his uncle, the elder Jones, were in business together, the elder Jones doing the buying of the antique tractors and motors, and then the selling of the finished products after the younger Jones rebuilt and refurbished them.

"'He was out there weed eating under the electric fence we used to hold the cows in,' the elder Jones said of his nephew. 'We didn't run cows, but we had some land, so we let another neighbor down the way from us use our land for *his* cows. We never even charged him a dime in rent. Hell, other neighbors who had large lots they weren't using for any particular reason all chipped in and let the man have their grass for hay. Steven would go cut it for him, since we had all those tractors, and whatnot. It was like one big neighborhood co-op. Everyone was helping everyone else in some way.'

"'Well, Steven had a weight problem,' the elder Jones shared with reporters. 'A little too much time sitting around on his backside fixing and rebuilding engines, and not enough time doing anything physical. He was working on it, and that's what he was doing out there that day, trying to help that other man, by making sure that the weeds weren't touching the wires on the fence, because that'll make the fence lose its charge, see, and a combination of the heat and Steven's health got to him, and he went into cardiac arrest. And that son of a (explicit) Gardener just stood over there and watched through his binoculars. Steven told me he was even calling out to the man for help, and still, he did nothing. Thank God Steven was able to get to his cell phone and call 911 himself, because that sick son of a (explicit) across the road never called them. It's like he was enjoying watching my nephew die.'

"The good news, according to the elder Jones, is not just that his nephew, Steven, lived, but that he took his heart attack as a wake up call and has completely transformed his life. 'He went to stay with his parents in Wisconsin once he got out of the hospital,' the elder Jones told reporters. 'Despite their age- they're in their seventies- they still run marathons. They'd always harped on Steven about his weight, and, well, I guess after the heart attack, he finally started listening to them. He's out there in Wisconsin still, and he's been running with his parents, and he's lost over one hundred pounds. He's completed two half marathons with his parents, and they're coming out here next spring to run the Marine Corp Marathon up in D.C., and then his parents are heading back out to Wisconsin, and Steven is going to stay on here and get back to work.

"'Fortunately,' the elder Jones added, 'I was able to make a couple of big sales while Steven was out there in Wisconscin getting healthy. He'd rebuilt two tractor motors from the 1920's inside the house of mine he lives in, and no, I don't charge him no rent, because he's family and all, and we split the proceeds from our business dealings- and I was able to sell those engines in Steven's absence. The buyers sent their own crews out to pick them up, and of course we've rebuilt the door frame to where you can take it off to move those big engines in and out of the house, because that's where Steven wanted his shop, right there in the living room. So we aren't hurting money wise. I tell you, I'm proud of my nephew and the transformation he's made with his life after his heart attack, but I sure as (explicit) don't thank that lunatic voyeur for any part of it. Good riddance to that hate filled son of a (explicit)!'

"It's a sad day for the LGBTQ community, the immigrant community and the minority communities not just of Albemarle County, Virginia today, but it is a sad day for the LGBTQ community , the immigrant community and the minority communities around the United States. Neo-Nazi, white suprimisist, homophobic, transgenderphobic, xeonophoic hate, which is spewed predominately by middle aged, conservative white males, has got to stop now or it never will. If you see something, say something!"

16

Later…

"Welcome back, peeps, it's your girl, Tania Tee in the house!"

(Crowd goes wild)

"Once again, you are all a part of the most *electrifying* internet podcast in the whole wide universe, and, Law'd, do we have a *show* for *you* tod*ay!*"

(Crowd goes wild)

"Ya'll remember that little girl that won America's Got Gumption? That cute little thang that made the sounds of all those different instruments with her mouth and her natural born voice? Remember her, ya'll?"

(Crowd goes wild)

"She won the championship round by putting it all together and came off sounding like a full orchestra playin' Bethoven's Fifth?

(Crowd goes wild)

"Well, she's here today, and she'll be performing live for us in the second half of the show!"

(Crowd goes wild)

"And we have funny man Chris Kringe here to entertain us in the middle of our show with his totally not safe work humor! Ya'll ready to cringe with Kringe?"

(Crowd goes wild)

"But first, we've got a panel here today, with whom we're gonna to have a bit of a more sombering conversation.

(Crowd is silent)

"Ya'll remember, three years ago now, what was billed back then as a murder suicide hate crime, when an alleged white, middle aged racist, homophobic, transgenderphobic and xoenophic man, Timothy Gardener, shot and killed a beautiful twenty eight year old transgender woman of Puerto Rican descent, Juanda Cruz, and then turned the gun on himself and comitted suicide?"

(Crowd moans with a mix of displeasure and sadness)

"Well, Tania Tee has a panel here today who's gonna try and tell us it's not what you think!"

(Crowd boos- some crowd members stand up and flip the bird and throw empty drink containers)

"Calm down, now. Calm down. Ya'll know Tania Tee screens her guests, and I wouldn't allow these people up here if their story didn't hold water."

(Crowd gasps and whispers in confusion)

"Hear these kind folks out. I spent time with them, getting to know them and hearing their story, and I *do* believe there's a message here. I just can't wrap my head around what that message is, and ya'll know Tania Tee has the smartest audience in all of podcast land, so Tania Tee's hoping ya'll can help me figure this out. Can ya'll help me?

(Crowd goes wild)

"Let's meet our guest panellists for today, going from left to right. First, we have Miss Billie G., who was Juanda's best friend."

(Crowd says "Hi, Miss Billie G." in unison)

"Ya'll makin' it feel like an AA meetin' up in here," Tania Tee says.

(Crowd laughs- except audience members who are in AA)

"Then we have Miss Julie and her husband Mike."

(Crowd greets Julie and Mike)

"Then we have Mr. Adam and his beautiful little daughter Mary Jane."

(Crowd greets Adam and Mary Jane)

"And then we have Mr. and Mrs. Overbaugh. Hey, should we wake him up, Mrs. Overbaugh?"

"No," says Mrs. Overbaugh. "You have to let him sleep it off."

(Crowd greets Overbaughs- sounding confused)

"And lastly, sitting on the end of our panel, we have Mr. Dr. Byron Blevens."

(Crowd greets Dr. Byron Blevins)

"Now, Mr. Dr. Blevins," Tania Tee says.

"Please," says Blevins. "Call me Byron."

"Okay, Byron," says Tania Tee. "So let me get this straight. Ya'll are here today to try to convince us that this tragedy that happened in ya'll's little community, just outside of Charlottesville, Virginia a few years back, was *not* a hate crime?"

"Yes," says Blevins.

(Crowd boos- some members stand and flip the bird and throw wadded up snack wrappers as they are now out of empty drink containers)

"Can we run the clip?" Blevins asks.

"Let's run the clip," Tania Tee says. "Audience, get ready to have your mind blown. Here's security camera footage taken from inside of Gardener's house on the night of the murder suicide. Tania Tee gonna warn ya, this is hard to watch. You might want to keep your eyes closed until after the first gunshot, but then you'd better open them eyes of ya'll's back up if you want to see the truth. Roll it, tech booth people."

(Clip rolls- footage shows post middle aged white male run into house, grab gun- warns pursuing woman to stop or he'll shoot- woman begins to speak, steps into house- post middle aged white male shoots pursuing woman in the forehead, killing her instantly- post middle aged white male searches for and then finds cellphone- calls 911- reports a murder and claims to have killed 'crazy Asian whore' in self defense- while talking to 911 operator, post middle aged white male bends over deceased woman lying on floor- lifts skirt- says "oh, shit" - pause- "holy fucking shit" and then puts barel of handgun in mouth and pulls trigger- falls to floor, dead instantly)

(Crowd draws in deep gasp of disbelief- has no words- no one stands, no one flips the bird- no one throws anything)

"Wow!" Tania Tee says. "Does that footage suggest what I think it suggests, Mr. Dr. Byron Blevins?"

"It does, indeed," Blevins says. "And for those of you in the audience who need it spelled out for you, or for those of you watching the livestream from home on your phones or computers who might need it spelled out for you, it's this; Timothy Gardener, honest to God, thought that Juanda Cruz was a biologically born woman and that his life was in danger. Not only did he think Juanda was a biologically born woman, but he thought, for some odd reason, that she was Asian, not Puerto Rican."

(Crowd gasps).

"Understand me," Blevins continues, while the crowd remains stunned, "we are *not* here to justify what Timothy Gardener did. We are *not* here to ask for forgiveness on his behalf. We are here to get the truth out."

"And what truth is that?" Tania Tee asks.

"We want to get the truth of Timothy's situation out to help other people who might be living in the same situation, for one," Blevins says, "but there is a point that we want to make *emphatically* clear, and that is that you cannot end hate with more hate. That's like trying to put out a fire by dousing it with gasoline, and there is far too much of that going on in our society, and no case in point better highlights this lunacy than the sad story of Timothy Gardener, a lunatic by all means, but certainly the best example we have for a case study for this argument."

"Okay," Tania Tee says. "You done lost Tania Tee, so I know you done lost half of Tania Tee's audience."

(Crowd laughs)

"So your saying this wasn't a hate crime carried out by some post middle aged backwoods hick who hated everyone who wasn't white, straight and protestant," Tania Tee says.

"Exactly," Blevins says. "Because other than being post middle aged and white and biologically male, Timothy Gardener was none of those other things. It might surprise you to know, as a matter of fact, that politically, he identified as a progressive liberal, and back before he lost his voting rights, he always voted straight ticket Democrat."

(Crowd gasps- a few members stand and boo- one audience member flips the bird- one digs into her purse to grab something to throw but she's already thrown her empty drink container and her empty snack wrapper so she resorts to flipping the bird)

"It's true," Julie says. "I was married to him for twelve years, and I knew him better than anyone else up here, but sadly, I have to admit that I didn't really know him at all."

"Tell us your side of the story, Miss Julie," Tania Tee says. "And by the way, audience, isn't Miss Julie one hot Momma?"

(Crowd goes wild and catcalls)

"You were Miss Teen Virginia first runner up when you were in high school, weren't you?" Tania Tee asks.

"Two years in a row, actually," Julie says. "I put myself through college modelling."

"And I hear you just got another contract," Tania Tee says.

"Yes," Julie says. "I retired from teaching a couple of years ago, and my pension only provides about sixty per cent of what I need to live, so I went to the mall one day to look for a part time job, and when I walked into a women's boutique, they were actually having a search for post middle aged models. When I walked in, the guy running the agency told his workers to take down all the contest advertisements and came running at me with a clipboard with a contract on it, and, well, I guess I found my part time job."

(Crowd goes wild- stands- catcalls)

"I'm very proud of my wife," Mike, sitting beside Julie, says.

"Now you hush up, you camel jockey, you," Tania Tee says. "You'll get your turn."

(Crowd laughs)

"What can you tell us about Timothy Gardener, your ex-husband?" Tania Tee asks.

"I can tell you," Julie says, "that though I was married to him for twelve years, and though I *thought* I knew him well, I didn't know him at all."

"Can you give us some details?" Tania Tee says. "Maybe some of the back history of your relationship?"

"Sure," Julie says. "I guess I'd gone to high school with him, but I don't remember him. He came up to me once, back when I was teaching at my old high school- he'd been demonstrating how to do something in shop class after having been asked to come in and do so by Mr. Henderson, our shop teacher, who I guess had had Timothy as a student. Mr. Henderson had heard about Timothy's recent felony conviction for bank fraud and he'd asked him to come in and show the kids how to do something to try to cheer him up. Mr. Henderson told me all of this after he saw me talking to Timothy in the hall that day. He warned me about him, about the felony and all that. He told me he wasn't a bad guy. He'd just slipped up. And he said he hadn't been a very good student, as far as the quality of his shop work went, but that he was a likeable guy, so he was trying to lift him up after what he'd been through.

"Anyway," Julie continues. "I'd just finalized my divorce from my first husband. I'm not proud of this, but I'll own up to it. I cheated on my first husband."

(Crowd lets out moan of disappointment)

"I know," Julie says. "Like I said, I'm not proud of it. It was a moment of weakness. I'd given birth to our second child, our son, about a year before, and I was still carrying around some baby fat, and I didn't feel very pretty. My husband was always working overtime. He was a cop, and he was out there dealing with crime crap all the time. Well, there was this cute new teacher at our school, and he was always giving me attention, and well, we fucked in the teachers lounge one day after school."

(Crowd stands and goes wild)

"I'm sorry," Julie says. "I didn't mean to use that language."

"Girl," Tania Tee says, "this here ain't *television*, this here's the *internet*. You say it how you *wanna* say it. *Fuck* the mother fuckin' FCC! They ain't the boss of Tania Tee!"

(Crowd- which is still still standing- continues to go wild)

"I hated telling my first husband about it, but I had to," Julie says. "My conscience was killing me. I didn't want to get divorced. I mean, I wanted us to work things out, but he couldn't get over what I'd done. He took it too personally. You see, he'd been in the Army, and he'd served in Iraq, and his truck team got hit by an I.E.D. He suffered severe burns, especially to his face, and he took it as if his physical appearance was the reason for my infidelity, but it wasn't."

"Ya'll know Tania Tee's stance on war and veterans," Tania Tee says. "She hate war, but she *love* the men and women who go fight in it so Tania Tee don't have to. Let's give a big round of applause for Miss Julie's first husband's service, even though he ain't here!"

(Crowd stands and goes wild)

"Thank you," Julie says. "And he's such a great guy. He forgave me, and he knew I didn't make much money as a teacher, and he knew I was pretty much paying out the nose there for a while to help my aged parents. They didn't have a lot of money, and they had to go into a facility when they were older- they've passed on now- and it was financially draining. And later, when I'd gotten remarried, and this would be to Timothy Gardener..."

(Crowd moans as if they'd just been group punched in the gut)

"... he knew Timothy didn't work or earn any income, so he always helped out. The court actually ruled that he would have custody of our children and receive support from *me*, but since he worked so much, he let the kids stay with me, and he even paid the equivalent of what he would have had to pay if he would have had to pay child support, because he knew I needed the money."

"Can we hear it for a real man?" Tania Tee says.

(Crowd stands and goes wild)

"My daughter stayed with her dad and his new wife most of the time, though," Julie says, "because her stepfather, Timothy Gardener, always gave her the creeps."

"Do you think that lunatic ever touched your children?" Tania Tee asks.

"No," Julie says. "It wasn't like that. And knowing what I know now, I think I would have had to have worried more about my son than my daughter. My daughter just always said that Timothy seemed angry, and like he was going to explode someday."

"Turns out your daughter was right," Tania Tee says.

"Not really," Byron Blevins cuts in. "This isn't a case so cut and dry."

"We'll come back to you, Mr. Dr. Byron Blevins," Tania Tee says. "You give Julie her turn."

"Yes, ma'am," Blevins says.

(Crowd giggles)

"You told me the story about your son, and the pornography, when we got together the first time, when I was screening ya'll for this show," Tania Tee says. "Can you tell our audience that part of your story?"

"Sure," Julie says. "As a mom, I'm always worried about what my kids might be doing online. So I was always doing history searches on our computer, to see who was looking at what. Well, I could tell that someone was erasing all their history. I assumed it was my son looking at porn, I mean, he *was* a teenager. It's what they do. They look at porn and eat junk food."

(Crowd laughs)

"Anyway," Julie continues. "I got on the computer one day to do a history search, and whoever had used it last had forgotten to clear their history. All that came up was porn site after porn site. I clicked on some of them, and it was all homosexual and transgender porn. Most of it, at least. There was actually some really sick stuff with animals on there."

(Crowd groans in disgust)

"I talked to Timothy about it," Julie says, "because of course, I'm assuming it was my son. And my thought process was that my son was gay. Which wouldn't have bothered me a bit if he was."

(Crowd cheers)

"And what did Timothy Gardener say?" Tania Tee asks.

"Pretty much what I just said," Julia says. "He's a teenager. They look at porn and eat junk food."

(Crowd laughs again- but not as much as first time- because everyone knows that funny things are never as funny the second time around)

"But it turns out, it *wasn't* your son looking at all of that, how shall I say it, eclectic pornography," Tania Tee says.

(Crowd chuckles)

"No," Julie says. "Because I finally approached my son. I wanted to talk to him about sexuality. I wanted to let him know that if he were attracted to other guys, or transgenders, that was okay by me, because he's my son, and I love him, and I wanted to let him know that I would support him in being *who* he was, no matter *who* that was."

(Crowd gives standing ovation)

"And that's when you found out it had been your husband at the time, Timothy Gardener, looking at that stuff?" Tania Tee says.

"Yes," Julie says. "My son laughed and told me it was Timothy. When I said I didn't believe him, my son got really serious. He looked me straight in the eyes, and he said, 'Mom, everyone knows your husband is gay except you.'"

(Crowd gasps)

"But it's more than that," Blevins shouts loudly over the crowd.

"You hush up, Mr. Dr. Byron Blevons, or Miss Tania Tee gonna come down there and give you a spankin'!" Tania Tee says.

"Please do," Blevins says.

(Crowd laughs)

"So what did you do then, armed with this new information," Tania Tee asks Julie.

"I decided to file for divorce," Julie says. "And not because of Timothy's sexuality, but because of all of it."

"And what is all of it?" Tania Tee asks.

"Mostly the lies and manipulations," Julie says. "He never worked. He claimed to be a boat builder, but he'd never built a boat in his life."

"What?" Tania Tee says. "All the papers said he built yachts."

"Yeah," Julie says. "The part they leave out is that he started to build a yacht something like fifteen years before his death, when he was married to his first wife, and he never finished it. He kept a somewhat mostly built hull of a yacht sitting around in a storage shed for going on two decades, and he told everyone he was a yacht builder. The fact was, the man never finished anything he started."

(Crowd moans in disapproval)

"It was all a facade," Julie says. "The man's entire life. He spent his life trying to convince people to see things in certain ways that simply weren't true, so they would never see him for who he truly was."

(Crowd moans empathetic "awe")

"When I talked to my son that day, about the porn," Julie continues, "he told me his sister had been *pleading* with him to go live with her and their father and step-mother, but my son confided in me that the reason he stayed with me, was because he was afraid Timothy was going to explode someday and hurt me. He stayed with me to protect me. He was a big kid, and a full grown man by the time I left Timothy. It was simply time to go. I mean, my son was playing bodyguard. That was sad and all I needed to know."

"So Timothy Gardener was a sociopath?" Tania Tee says.

"But it's more than that," Blevins says, emphatically.

(Tania Tee walks down stage- motions for Byron Blevins to stand, turn and bend over- he does- Tania Tee smacks him on the ass- crowd laughs)

"Thank you, may I have another?" Blevins says, returning to his seat.

(Crowd laughs)

"He was definitely sociopathic," Julie says. "But Byron convinced me, like he's been saying here, there was a lot more to it than that. It wasn't just the lying and the manipulation of me and my kids," Julie adds. "He did it with everyone. He would put words in my friends' mouths and then accuse them of being things they weren't. Hell, the last day I was in that house, he gave me a slip of paper that had the name and phone number of a battered womens and children's shelter downtown on it and he demanded I take it over and give it to these wonderful, wonderful people sitting here beside me," Julie says, motioning toward Adam, a middle aged white male, and Mary Jane, a twenty year old Filipina woman. "Timothy told me some white suprimicist Nazy and his mail order bride had just moved in beside him, and that we needed to make sure the poor girl knew that men weren't allowed to mistreat women in this country, and he wanted to make sure she knew where to go for help."

"Did you deliver the name and number of the center to the new neighbors?" Tania Tee asks.

"I did no such *thing*," Julie says. "I went over there and introduced myself to these wonderful people, and I quickly found out their relationship was *nothing* like what my lunatic ex-husband *thought* it was. But I wasn't surprised. I mean, by this time, he'd lost his mind completely. He had no idea what reality was."

"So he was delusional? Maybe even schizophrenic?" Tania Tee asks.

"It's more…" Blevins begins, but trails off after receiving a stern look from Tania Tee.

(Crowd giggles)

"We'll come back to you later, Miss Julie," Tania Tee says. "Let's move on to Mr. Adam and Miss Mary Jane, here. How are ya'll today?"

"Good," Adam and Mary Jane say in unison. "Thanks for having us," Adam says.

"Adam, what is your relationship with this beautiful young lady sitting with you here today?" Tania Tee asks.

"She's my daughter," Adam says.

(Crowd stairs in silence- faces filled with confusion)

"Can't you tell?" Adam says, leaning over and putting one arm around Mary Jane, beside him, and pulling her toward him. "She looks just like me!"

(Crowd bursts into laughter)

"Mary Jane," Tania Tee says. "How old are you?"

"I'm twenty."

"And are you in college?"

"I *am*," Mary Janes says. "I'm studying English as a second language at the University of Virginia in Charlottesville."

(A lone crowd member stands and shouts "Go Hoos, Go!"- rest of crowd looks at him with blank expressions)

"Why did you pick English as a second language?" Tania Tee asks.

"When I came here from the Philippines," Mary Jane says, "I knew very little English. I had good teachers, and I learned quickly, but as a person from another, non-English speaking country, who came here at a young age and learned to speak English after getting here, I feel I can help others in that same position get over the learning curve a lot quicker."

"How old were you when you came here from the Philippines?" Tania Tee asks.

"Four," Mary Jane says.

"So you were married to Mary Jane's mother, right?" Tania Tee says to Adam.

"Yes," Adam says. "I was a writer for the VA in Manilla. I'd actually spent a year in Iraq as an embedded journalist. I was with an infantry unit in Mosul, but I want to make it very clear to everyone here and now, I was *never* a member of the U.S. armed forces. I was part of a group of journalists who actually went to basic training with a unit, followed them through to their active duty station, and then went on deployment with them. We documented their experience from day one of basic training through their deployment, and then that's how I ended up writing for the VA. Contacts I made through that experience. But I *never* served, and I am *not* a veteran."

"Wow!" Tania Tee says. "But it sounds like you pretty much are. Like, you pretty much did the same thing."

"No!" Adam says, emphatically. "You are either a veteran or you are not. There is no such thing as 'pretty much the same thing' when it comes to being a veteran. And that's one of the things that lunatic, Timothy Gardener, never understood. But we'll get to that."

"Okay, Mr. Adam," Tania Tee says, " but how is what you went through *not* pretty much the same thing, if you're over there getting shot at with them and all that?" Tania Tee asks.

"Because when we were getting shot at," Adam says, "I was hiding under tables, behind vehicles, or anywhere else I could find to hide, praying to the God of my understanding to get us out of there alive, while these brave men and women- and yes, there were women attached to our unit fighting as well- were taking the fight to the enemy. Sure, we got out of those situations, because God answered my prayers, but we also got out of those situations, because those badass American soldiers, men *and* women, kicked the living shit out of those terrorist bastards!"

(Crowd stands and goes wild- several crowd members cry)

"So tell us how this beautiful young lady beside you came into your life," Tania Tee says, after the crowd's enthusiasm subsides and they return to their seats.

"I met and fell in love with her mother when I was working for the VA as a writer in Manilla," Adam says. "Her mother, Judy, was actually a security guard at the VA. Every morning when I showed up for work, she would pat me down to make sure I wasn't carrying a bomb or a gun, and I'd always smile while she did it, and when she was done, I'd tell her, 'no. don't stop. Keep going.'"

(Crowd laughs)

"*Da*-ad," Mary Jane says, sounding embarrassed. Adam looks at her and mouths the word 'sorry.'

"I'd go out and talk to her when I was on my breaks," Adam continues, "and I finally asked her out, and in a short time we were dating, and, well, Mary Jane here was two years old at the time. Her biological father wasn't in the picture, so I kinda stepped into that role, and next thing you know, we're one happy little family, and when my time was up working for the VA I brought Judy and Mary Jane back to the U.S. with me, and we bought a small piece of land, two acres, on the James River, in the southern part of the county, outside of Charlottesville, a little town called Scottsville, and it was our plan to live there, happily ever after."

"But happily ever after didn't last," Tania Tee says. "Tragedy struck."

"It did," Adam says. "Mary Jane's mother, Judy, was killed in an ATV accident about six years ago."

(Crowd moans a sad 'awe')

"And then, I understand," Tania Tee says, "a *real* nightmare began for you and your daughter?"

"That's right," Adam says. "The insurance company, though never accusing, *insinuated* that there was 'foul play' in regard to my wife's death, and they launched an investigation that lasted *forever*. They just didn't want to pay out the death benefit- I mean, they *are* an insurance company. They take your money for your premiums, but when they owe *you*, they never want to pay- so anyway, it did become a nightmare. It didn't help that people started talking, thinking maybe there was truth to the insinuation. You know, American guy marries an immigrant woman, brings her to the U.S., insures her life, and then kills her. Sounded like the perfect television crime. All those shows based on that stuff that people stay glued to didn't help."

"But the rumors didn't just stop there, did they?" Tania Tee says.

"Oh, no," Mary Jane says. "I could hear the kids whispering at school. They thought my dad killed my mom so he could be with me. 'You know how those Filipinas are,' I'd hear them say. 'They're all whores.'"

(Crowd moans an empathetic "awe")

"We actually moved to the opposite end of the county for Mary Jane's last couple of years in high school," Adam adds. "To get her into a new school and out of that situation. I felt so bad for her. Anyway, that's how we ended up being neighbors with Timothy Gardener."

"And what were your thoughts on Timothy Gardener?" Tania Tee asks.

"Well," Adam begins, "Julie kind of warned us a little bit that day she came over and met with us. She gave us her name and number on a slip of paper and said we were free to call her anytime if we ever needed anything. Talking to her off and on as Timothy showed, well, signs of being a fucking lunatic, helped, but I *always* felt uncomfortable around him."

"*You*," Mary Jane says, looking over at her father. "What about *me*?" Mary Jane shivers, as if a goose just walked over her grave.

"Oh," Adam says. "She had it *worse*." He nods his head toward his daughter. "He was always making these off-color cracks about Chinese people when he'd come over. It was, like, how he'd drum up a conversation.

"And I could see the way he *looked* at her. I wanted to tell her to maybe cover up a little more skin when we were outside, but *she* wasn't the one being inappropriate. She was just a teenager out in the Virginia summer heat, so I couldn't ask her to be miserable because our neighbor was a perverted voyeur. I mean, we could always see him over there watching us. It was really creepy. It's like he never even tried to *hide* it. But what was worse, were times when he'd come over, always uninvited, and just start talking *at* us."

"Talking *at* you," Tania Tee says. "You explained this to me during our interview. Can you tell our audience what you mean by talking *at* you?"

"Sure," Adam says. "It's like, the man would come over, and he'd usually start out with some kind of meaningless smalltalk that usually involved something very inappropriate, and then, you could tell, when you were talking to him, that he absolutely was *not* listening. He never made eye contact. He just kind of stared at the ground, and he seemed completely uninterested in what you were saying. It's like he was just thinking about what *he* was going to say next. The only time he wasn't looking down at the ground is when he was looking at my daughter, like he wanted to rape her, and by the way, she was underage most the time that we lived beside him."

"So the man was pedophelic?" Tania Tee says.

"No," Byron Blevins says. "It's more…"

(Crowd gives Blevins stern look- Blevins shuts up)

"And no matter what he told you, his story was always changing," Adam continues. "He'd tell you one thing one day, then something completely different the next."

"So he was a gaslighter," Tania Tee says, "and Mr. Dr. Byron Blevins, don't you even *think* about opening that mouth of yours, or Miss Tania Tee gonna come down there and smack it!"

(Crowd laughs)

"I don't know what he was," Adam says, "other than a true lunatic."

"Now, you told me during the interview," Tania Tee says, "that you felt the man came to hate you. Could you tell our audience about that?"

"Sure," Adam says. "I mean, I never had anything against the man. Except for how he looked at my daughter, and all the racist Asian and antisemetic jokes he'd crack. I called him out on the Asian stuff once, and some of the antisemetic stuff he'd say, and he'd tell me that he was a progressive liberal or some crap, and that it wasn't possible for him to be racist or antisemetic. I told him that I didn't think he was quite as progressive as he thought he was, and that's where it all started. Him not liking me. Well, that and the time I got in his face for claiming to be a veteran when he wasn't."

"He did *what!*" Tania Tee shouts in anger.

(Crowd boos loudly)

"Yeah," Adam says. "I guess he'd been in R.O.T.C. while he was in college, and he claims that that's the same thing as having served in the Navy, so he claimed to be a veteran."

"What?" Julie cuts in. "You mean that son of a bitch was never actually in the Navy?"

"You didn't *know*?" Tania Tee asks Julie.

"*Hell* no!" Julie says. "I actually volunteered to help out with a veterans group at my church from time to time, because I thought he had served in the Navy, and because I actually support veterans. He would go with me and rub elbows with the veterans that would show up, and go on and on about his Navy days while speaking with them."

"You honest to *God* didn't know?" Tania Tee says.

"I'm not making this up," Julie says.

"There will be a *lot* about this man's life coming out over the coming years that most people didn't know," Blevins says. "Fifty six years worth of lies cannot all be exposed in only a few short years."

"Miss Tania Tee gonna let you get away with that one, Mr. Dr. Byron Blevins, but you best hush up!"

(Crowd laughs)

"Anyway," Adam goes on. "I always felt sorry for the guy. He was always alone. No one ever came to see him. Like, the only people we ever saw over there were delivery guys, and he was usually yelling at them. The man was *not* stable.

"He'd come over when we'd be doing yard work, and he'd lament about how he couldn't afford to pay to have his yard work done, and of how he didn't have the equipment to do it. We figured he was lying about the equipment part…"

"He was," Julie breaks in. "I bought him everything he needed to take care of our lot, but he was just too lazy to get up off his ass and go outside and do it."

"We kind of figured," Adam says. "I mean, it didn't take long to figure out that nothing the man ever said was true. But we felt sorry for him, so we'd do some of it for him from time to time. I just always kind of felt like maybe he wouldn't be so bad off if he just had someone who was nice to him.

"But anyway, I guess he decided he hated us once we'd garnered a little bit of success on YouTube. Well, I'll let Mary Jane take over here, because I don't even understand how that social media thing works. I just know how to push record on the iphone. She does all the rest."

(Crowd laughs)

"We were struggling with money," Mary Jane says. "Dad was paying a mortgage on our place down in Scottsville, and he was paying rent on our house in White Hall, where we were renting. I felt bad about it, because I knew I was the reason we'd moved. All the rumors at my old school."

"Where the hell am I!" Mr. Overbaugh shouts from out of nowhere, having woken up suddenly from sleeping the sleep of the dead and not recognizing his surroundings.

"Go back to sleep, dear," Mrs. Overbagh, sitting beside him, says. "It ain't our turn yet."

"Oh," Mr. Overbaugh says. He slumps back down in his chair and goes back to sleep.

(Crowd stares with crinkled faces- a look of *what the fuck* written all over them)

"Anyway," Mary Jane continues, "I knew a few kids from school, my old school, who had YouTube channels. And they were actually making money. So I started a YouTube channel and I roped my dad into making videos with me, and damn, if we didn't end up going *viral!* Money wasn't a problem anymore, and the insurance company ended up paying out and leaving us alone, finally, and I'd graduated from high school and started school at U.V.A., so we moved back to our place in Scottsville. Sure, some of our neighbors down there still whispered if they saw us, but having lived beside that creeper Timothy Gardener for three years let us view our neighbors in Scottsville in a different light. They were small fry compared to *that* lunatic. And they kept to themselves. They might have been gossiping about us, but they left us the hell alone. Never took it upon themselves to come waltzing over to our place and just start chatting us up just to see *what* we were doing, under the guise of asking us *how* we were doing."

"Ain't that just the oldest nosy neighbor trick in the book?" Tania Tee says. "Acting like they give a damn *how* you're doing when you know all they really wanna know is *what* you're doing?"

(Crowd nods and says 'uh-huh')

"Now tell us about this YouTube thing ya'll got goin'," Tania Tee says.

"We started out just making gardening videos," Adam says. "I was having a hard time getting freelance work as a writer. I mean, that's how far and wide the rumors about my wife's death had spread. It's like I had leprosy. No one wanted to touch me."

"I can't imagine," Tania Tee says. "You lose the person you love most in life, and then you get treated like it's somehow your fault. Like *you're* the bad guy."

"Exactly," Adam says. "I'd liken it to a parent who has their children stolen from them by an ex-spouse, or kidnapped by a stranger, and then being viewed by everyone around them as the reason it happened. Like, maybe if they'd have hired a better lawyer, or if they would have paid closer attention it wouldn't have happened. You get to suffer loss and experience grief while being guilt shamed all at the same time. Winner winner, chicken dinner."

"I'm so sorry you went through that," Tania Tee says.

"Thank you," Adam says. "Anyway, Mary Jane convinced me to try this YouTube thing. So we'd make videos of us gardening. I think at first, most people just watched becasue Mary Jane is so damn cute."

"Awe, Daddy," Mary Jane says, and she slaps her father on the arm.

(Crowd moans "awe" in adoration)

"Anway, we hit paydirt when we planted a cherry tree in the yard on the anniversary of Judy's passing. We called Mr. and Mrs. Overbaugh here, of course, and asked permission." Adam nods toward the older couple toward the end of the panel, sitting just before Byron Blevins. "They were our landlords. They owned the property, so we had to ask. They lived back through the woods a way behind us.

"Anyway," Adam continues, "we made a video about that, and all these people, our viewers, started commenting about people they'd lost, and they were asking if we'd plant a tree for them and make a video about it. I called the Overbaughs again, and told them I had a weird request, but they said it was okay."

"What did you think when you got that request, Mrs. Overbaugh?" Tania Tee asks the old lady toward the end of the panel.

"I thought it was a great idea," Mrs. Overbagh says. "Mr. Overbagh, here, and I, lost a child. Our son drowned when he was six years old. He was our only child. Why, we asked Adam to plant a tree in honor of our son's memory, and he sure did."

"So you owned, at one point, Mrs. Overbaugh, the property that Timothy Gardener bought and built his house on, is that correct?" Tania Tee asks.

"No!" Julie says, breaking in. "The Overbaughs owned the land that *Julie, then* Gardener, *now* Black, bought and built the house on. That deadbeat *Timothy* Gardener never paid for *anything*!"

"It's okay, dear," Mr. Black, Julie's current husband says, patting her on the arm. "Julie's just…"

"You hush up, Mr. Camel Jockey!" Tania Tee says. "We'll get to you."

(Crowd gives a nervous giggle)

"Yes, we owned the land," Mrs. Overbagh says. "My husband and I only had one child, and like I said, he died when he was six. All we had after that was ourselves, and that was okay. We both came from abusive homes, and we were really looking forward to loving our little guy in such a way we'd never been loved, but God had other plans for us."

"And what were those plans?" Tania Tee asks.

"To love others," Mrs. Overbagh says. "Unconditionally. And to help as many people as we could."

"And how have you done that?" Tania Tee asks.

"We started to invest what little we had in real estate," Mrs. Overbaugh says. "And this was way back, before the Charlottesville area exploded with growth. We made far more money than we needed, so we'd donate land. We'd sell land and donate the proceeds to good causes. Anyway, we felt we could help, and that's why we gave the money to build the camp down at…"

"Nah, ah, ah," Tania Tee cuts in. "Not just yet. We'll get to that. Can you tell us about your husband's condition? I know our audience has *got* to be wondering why the man's sitting there sleeping, like he's passed out drunk."

"Oh, no," Mrs. Overbaugh says, giggling. "He ain't passed out drunk. Mr. Overbaugh's a good Christian man. He might take a nip every now and then, but he's never been drunk in his life. Just like it says in the good book, "be ye not filled with wine where it is in excess, but be filled with the spirit of the Lord."

(Crowd looks on in silence- faces blank- a lone cricket that had somehow made its way into the studio chirps from backstage- everyone in attendance hears it)

"Your husband's condition, Mrs. Overbaugh?" Tania Tee says.

"Oh," Mrs. Overbaugh says. "He has narcolepsy. Why, sometimes he goes out for walks and falls asleep in the middle of the woods, and I have to go out and find him."

(Crowd moans an understanding "awe")

"Did your dealings with Timothy Gardener end after he bought, rather," Tania Tee says, catching herself, and then looking down at Julie, who's giving her a look that says, 'you'd *better* reword what you're saying, Tania Tee!' "Did your dealings with Timothy Gardener come to an end after Julie bought the land from you guys?"

"Absolutely *not*," Mrs. Overbaugh says. "They were just *beginning*. The man was calling me day in and day out to tell me every little thing any of our renters who were renting our house over there beside him were doing. I eventually just stopped answering the phone when he called. I'd recognize his number on the caller i.d., and I wouldn't touch it!

"That old house, by the way, was built in 1903," Mrs. Overbagh adds, "and it's the house I grew up in and it's the house my daddy grew up in. My family lost it on the auction block at one point when they fell on hard times back in the seventies, you know, when that peanut farmer was in office and destroyed the economy, but just as soon as I could when me and Mr. Overbaugh started making money investing in real estate, in the eighties, once that good lookin' movie star got up in there and fixed everything, why, I bought the house back to get it back in the family."

"That's an endearing story," Tania Tee said. "But back to this YouTube thing," she says, turning to face Adam and Mary Jane again. "Tell us more about it."

"Well," Adam says, "we were planting trees for all these people making requests, and the channel was growing, and we ended up getting monetized and making a little money, and then, well, Jeromy's camel, Sally, stuck her head through the treeline one day when we were filming a video, and man, everything just blew up big from there."

"Okay, Mr. Camel Jockey," Tania Tee says. "Now it's your turn. Tell us your story."

"Hi everyone, I'm Jeromy."

(Hi Jeromy the crowd says in unison)

"Wow," Jeromy says. "It really *is* like an AA meeting."

(Crowd chuckles- but not those who are in AA- and not as much as when Tania Tee said this at the beginning of the show, being that this was the second time around)

"So, I met Adam and his daughter because of Sally. They used to pet her on the head and stuff when she'd stick her head through the treeline on the border of the property. I went out to find her one day, and they were there with her, and we started talking…"

"Wait a minute," Tania Tee says. "Don't you know how to tell a story? You gotta start at the beginning. How in the name of all things holy did you end up with a camel named Sally?"

"It's a sad story, really," Jeromy says. "Years ago, my wife and I- my first wife (he gives a nervous glance to Julie)- us and our little girl, Amanda, had gone up to the zoo in D.C. My wife and I were about thirty at the time, and Amanda was four. Well, Amanda fell in love with a camel we saw that day, and on the way home, she was telling me she wanted a camel. 'Daddy, buy me a camel,' she kept demanding. 'We'll name her Sally. And she has to have two humps.' Well, when we were almost home, we were in an accident. A tractor trailer being driven by a drunk driver ran through a redlight. Smacked right into us. My wife and daughter were killed instantly. I spent a month in a coma and then six months in the hospital after that."

(Crowd moans a heartbroken "awe")

"Anyway," Jeromy continues. "Long story short, when I got out of the hospital and got the life insurance payout, it felt like blood money to me. I didn't want it. So I used it all to buy the land I bought out in White Hall, and I looked and looked and looked, and I finally found a two hump camel that needed a good home. She was a retired movie star."

"What?" Tania Tee says.

(What?- the crowd says in unison)

"Yeah," Jeromy says. "She was used in movies. Like, she was in Jumanji and the Gladiator. A few others."

"You're *kidding*," Tania Tee says. "I mean, you told me this during our original interview, but this is still so neat it sounds almost unbelievable."

"I know, right?" Jeromy says. "So, her trainer had retired her, and they were going to send her to some reserve in Washington state that's home to retired animal actors, but I was able to purchase her for a reasonable price and honor my daughter Amanda's last request."

(Crowd moans a heartwarming "awe")

"And now you're married to Julie," Tania Tee says. "How did that happen?"

"Well," Julie says. "I used to go over there and pet Sally when I lived a couple of properties over. That's how I got to know Jeromy. After my divorce, well, I guess I just kept going over to see Sally. At least that's the *excuse* I'd use. But I was really going over to see Jeromy. He always had this sweet, loveable aura about him, and I knew about his family, because he'd told me. I don't know," Julie says, looking over at Jeromy. "We fell in love, and, well, you know the rest."

(Crowd moans an adorable "awe")

"Out of curiosity," Tania Tee says, "what was Timothy Gardener's opinion of Jeromy's camel?"

"Oh," Julie says, "the first time I saw Sally out one of our windows, I said, 'Tim, I think that guy over there has a camel,' and he says, 'yeah, I'm sure he's probably fucking it.'"

"Are you *serious*?" Tania Tee says.

"Yes," Julie says. "That was his MO. Always thinking the worst of everyone and every situation."

"So he was a pessimist," Tania Tee says. "And Mr. Dr. Byron Blevins, don't you *even* tell us there's more to it, because we know, and you're gonna get your chance at the end."

(Crowd laughs)

"Very *much* a pessimist," Julie says. "He could have won the lottery and all he would have done would be bitch about the taxes he had to pay on the winnings."

"Now, tell us what Sally the two humped camel did for your YouTube channel, Mary Jane," Tania Tee says.

"Like my dad said," Mary Jane says. "Our channel blew up. We started going viral. People were saying in the comment section that there was a Bigfoot Sasquatch just inside the treeline of our videos watching what we were doing. We actually would go back and watch our videos, looking at the time stamps and everything. We couldn't see any Bigfoot Sasquatch."

(Crowd laughs at the idea of Bigfoot Sasquatch *actually* being real)

"We started making videos where we'd go out into the woods that separated the property we were renting from Jeromy's property," Adam adds, "looking for this Bigfoot Sasquatch that, potentially, lived in the woods behind our house. Man, we got such a huge following, and people kept saying they were seeing Bigfoot Sasquatch, but Mary Jane and I would go back over the footage and all we'd see, every now and then, was Sally the two humped camel either walking around on the other side of the property line or sticking her big pretty head into the woods to eat leaves from the trees."

"I asked my dad once," Mary Jane says, "do you think they're seeing Sally? And they think she's a Bigfoot Sasquatch?"

"I told her *no way*," Adam says. "That's freaking *crazy*."

"We *never* understood where the whole Bigfoot Sasquatch thing was coming from," Mary Jane continues, "but it drew a crowd, and people kept asking us to plant trees in honor of lost loved ones, and before we knew it, Dad didn't have to worry about finding writing jobs anymore."

"I had no idea how much money you could make on YouTube," Adam says. "Anyway, that brings us back to our story. That lunatic from next door comes over one day, making some quasi-racist, quasi-pedophilic jokes about my daughter, and then he straight out asks me how much money we were making on YouTube. I told him, and he lost his shit. I mean, I always had a feeling he hated successful people, which isn't uncommon among deadbeats, and I guess this confirmed it."

"He hated everybody, because he hated himself," Byron Blevins said, not thinking, and then he dropped to his knees and begged Tania Tee for forgiveness.

"I'll forgive you, as long as you don't say another mother lovin' word until it's your turn to speak again," Tania Tee said.

(Crowd laughs)

"Anyway," Adam continues, "he asked me if I was familiar with West Virginia. He always asked me that over and over, and like I'd told him a million times before, I was not *from* West Virginia. Sure, I'd been over there. When Judy was alive, she and Mary Jane and I used to drive over there in the fall to look at the leaves after they'd changed colors. But once again, I told him many times I was from Coeur D'Alene, Idaho. But like I said earlier, you could tell whenever you talked to this guy, he wasn't listening. It's like, he was just thinking about what he was going to say next.

"So, he goes off on some tangent about how much he hated Chuck Yaeger," Adam continues, "and calls him a dumb hillbilly and says it does't matter how much success one garners, if they're from West Virginia, they'll never be anything but a dumb hillbilly. Well, I just stared at him, wondering where it had all come from, and what it had to do with me, because like I said, I'm originally from Coeur D'Alene, Idaho. But I wasn't surprised the man's gibberish wasn't making any sense. It never did."

"Do ya'll know where Miss Tania Tee from?" Tania Tee says, addressing the audience.

(No- the crowd says in unison)

"Tania Tee from a little timber town called Deadwood, West Virginia."

(Crowd gasps)

"Tania Tee look like a dumb hillbilly to any ya'll?"

(No- the crowd says- some members booing at the thought)

"Tania Tee done went and grew up a poor little black girl stuck in a poor little black boy's body down there in West Virginia."

(Crowd giggles)

"And you know how them so called *dumb hillbillies* in West Virginia treated Tania Tee?"

(Crowd sits silently with blank expressions on their faces)

"Like Tania Tee one of they own!"

(Crowd goes wild)

"Those people over there the salt of the earth. And if'n you tried to step up and hurt Tania Tee? Or you tried to badmouth Tania Tee for being who she is? They'd give you a good 'ol fashioned country ass whoopin'!"

(Crowd rises to its feet in applause)

"Um, hello," the lone panelist who hadn't spoken yet says. "Are we gonna sit here and talk about camels and Bigfoots and hillbillies all day? Or can we talk about my best friend for a few minutes?"

"Sorry, girl," Tania Tee says. "I was fixin' to get to you. Everybody, say hello to Miss Billie G."

(Crowd says- 'Hello, Billy G.')

"What were you all saying about an AA meeting earlier?" Billie G. says.

(Crowd does not laugh at all- *especially* members who really are in AA- because by the third time around, *nothing* is funny anymore)

"Folks," Tania Tee says, "Billie G. was best friends with Juanda Cruz. Billie G., can you tell us about your relationship with Juanda? How you met? All of it?"

"Sure," Billie G. says. "I met Juanda when she still went by Juan. Juan came to me for a job interview about three years before he, rather, *she* was murdered by that lunatic that lived across the road from me."

"A job interview," Tanie Tee says. "Tell us about where you work."

"I work for the largest BMW dealership in central Virginia," Billie G. says. "I started in sales, but I worked my way up to sales manager. Juanda, who was still Juan at the time, was looking for a job."

"And you hired him? I mean, her?" Tania Tee says.

"Yes," Billie G. says. "I hired *him*, but I knew I was really hiring *her*."

"Can you explain what you mean by that, Miss Billie G.?" Tania Tee says.

"Yes," Billie G. says. "When I met Juan, he thought he was a gay man. But I could see who Juan really was, and I knew that Janda was in there trying to get out."

"And how did you know this?" Tania Tee asks.

"Because once upon a time," Billie G. says, "I was Billie B. As in Billy *Boy*. It's what my father called me, because *he* knew before I ever did *something* was different with me. And he didn't want me to figure it out. So he was always reiterating my wrongfully assigned birth gender. Like he was trying to drill it in my brain before I had a chance to figure it out."

"But you figured it out," Tania Tee says. "Like we all do, eventually."

(Crowd goes wild)

"Yes," Billie G. says, "and I never held back. I had gender reassignment surgery about a decade ago, and to celebrate the true me finally being released, I started going by Billie G. for Billie Girl, because that is who I really am!"

(Crowd goes wild)

"And you could tell Juan was Juanda?" Tania Tee says.

"I could," Billie G. says. "I didn't see the package, I saw the person."

"It's called Pangender," Byron Blevins said. "It's what I'm trying to tell you people."

"Mr. Dr. Byron Blevins, do I need to tell you to hush up in a different language for you to understand me?" Tania Tee says.

(Crowd laughs)

"Mary Jane," Tania Tee says, facing the young Filipina woman. "Do you still speak Tagalog? Can you tell Mr. Dr. Byron Blevins to shut up in Tagalog?

(Crowd laughs)

"Sure," Mary Janes says, smiling. She turns and faces Blevins, stops smiling, and yells, "pag he-lum!"

(Crowd laughs hysterically)

"Please continue, Billie G." Tania Tee says.

"That's really all there is to it," Billie G. says. "We became best of friends, and once, when she needed a place to stay, because her lease was up on her apartment in town and she wanted to save money on rent, I suggested the big old farm house across the road from my place. It gave her a longer drive to work, but it was five hundred dollars a month cheaper in rent. I would have never suggested it though if I would have realized how much of a lunatic that man living up there in the house above it was."

"Did you ever have any dealings with Timothy Gardener?" Tania Tee asks.

"Only once," Billie G. says. "I mean, I always saw him up there looking around at everyone and everything they had going on with his binoculars. I heard about what the prick did when that sweet man next door had his hard attack. It didn't surprise me.

"But anyway, once, while Adam and Mary Jane were still renting over there, I'd come home from work, and I'd gotten out of the demo I was driving- that's one of the perks to my job, I don't have to have a car payment myself, because I get to drive demos- so I get out to open my gate- I allowed a friend of mine who had a couple of horses to keep her horses at my place, off and on, when she'd go on vacation and whatnot- and I look over, and he's standing across the road just staring. Well, I thought maybe he liked the car, so I asked him if he liked what he saw. I mean, I'm always selling. You don't move your way up to sales manager because you're not, you know.

"Anyway, he almost had a damn *meltdown*. Starts telling me he's not rich like everyone else, and he couldn't afford it. Hell, we sell BMWs to teachers. I mean, they have to finance them out for eight years. No offense, Julie," Billie G. says, leaning forward and peering down the row of guests to face Julie.

"You don't have to tell *me*," Julie says.

"Anyway," Billie G. continues, "I told him I might be able to come down on price for such a nice guy like him. I mean, the guy gave me the creeps, but you'll never close a sale by telling someone they give you the creeps."

(Crowd laughs)

"But he just stomped off, complaining about rich people, or something, and that's both the first and last time I ever talked to him."

"I know this is going to be painful," Tania Tee says. "But can we fast forward? Can you take us to that fateful night when you lost your best friend?"

"Sure," Billie G. says, sitting up stoically, and then automatically slumping over and bursting into tears.

(Crowd moans a heartbreaking "awe")

"Her parents were so proud of her," Billie G. says, speaking and crying into tissues a stage hand gives her. "They came here from Puerto Rico with nothing but the shirts on their backs. Juanda was born here, and they worked so hard to give her a good life- a life like they never had growing up back in their homeland- and when I went with her to tell them she was going to have gender reassignment surgery, and she'd come to that decision on her own, I didn't coax her- they both hugged her and told her they loved her, and they cried tears of happiness."

(Crowd moans a heartfelt "awe")

"She was doing good at her job," Billie G. says. "She had a boyfriend who was in full support of her decision."

"Where is he now?" Tania Tee asks.

"He was all torn up," Billie G. says. "He lived in a bottle for the first year after her murder, but he's since gotten sober. He's in A.A."

(Crowd laughs hysterically- except those really in AA)

"You sick bastards!" Tania Tee shouts at the crowd.

"No," Billie G. says. "It's okay. That was pretty fucking funny."

(Crowd laughs again, but not hysterically)

"We celebrated her decision on that fateful night," Billie G. continues. "Since it was Halloween, we decided to do it Samhain style."

"Sam who?" Tania Tee says.

"You really *are* from West Virginia, *aren't* you?" Blevins says.

(Crowd laughs)

"You know," Billie G. says. "The original Celctic harvest festival, which would go on to become Halloween?"

"Tania Tee know *exactly* what *Samhain* mean," Tania Tee says, shooting a dirty look at Byron Blevins. "Don't you be pulling them dumb hillbilly joks on Tania Tee Mr. Dr. Byron Blevins."

(Crowd laughs)

"We decided we would burn any personal effects of *Juan* Cruz," Billie G. said. "Any of his old clothes. Anything that represented who *Juanda* Cruz was *not*. To us, that night marked the turning point. Juan Cruz was dead. He would never see another sunrise, and we were shouting this at the top of our lungs. It was such an emotional release. From that moment forward, Juanda was Juanda, no matter *what* some heterosexually/homosexually/bisexually only minded doctor proclaimed her to be when she entered the world bearing a set of genitals she never asked for.

"After we'd burned the last of Juans effects, we hugged and kissed, and said goodnight, and that was the last time I ever saw my best friend. Alive, at least."

"As painful as it is," Tania Tee says, "can you tell us what happened next?"

"Yeah," Billie G. says, crying anew. "I walked down the long driveway to the road, crossed the road, and then started up my driveway. For a minute, I thought I heard Juanda scream. Something like, 'you sick fucker.' I just thought maybe she was releasing some rage toward Juan, you know, for keeping her trapped for nearly thirty years. But then, about a minute later, when I heard the gunshot, I knew something terrible had happened."

"What did you think had happened?" Tania Tee asks.

"Well, I was certain it had *something* to do with that sick lunatic next door, Timothy Gardener. I called 911 on my cellphone to report the gunshot I'd heard, I gave the address, and then I took off running as fast as I could. I got back to the fire, but I didn't see Juanda. Then, I heard the second gunshot up at the lunatic's house. I ran up there, not realizing how *dumb* it actually was to do so. I mean, I had no idea he'd taken himself out with that second shot. He could have been shooting her a second time. I've played it through a million different ways in my head. I'm lucky I didn't get killed that night."

"And what did you see when you got to the house?" Tania Tee asks.

"I saw my best friend," Billie G. says, fighting back yet *another* round of tears.

"Take your time," Tania Tee says.

After a moment, Billie G. says, "I saw my best friend, lying there, dead. She had a bullet hole in her forehead, and her skirt had been pulled up. I thought maybe it just rose up when she fell, until the first time I saw the tape you started the show with today.

"And I saw that sick fucker who murdered her lying there, dead, too. He had a huge hole in the back of his head, and there was blood everywhere, and I don't really remember the next few minutes, but I can remember being in the yard, throwing up, and a police officer coming over and asking me if I was okay. I looked up, and I thought it was all a dream, because it looked like the officer was wearing a mask, or something. Then I remembered it was Halloween. And I thought the officer was… I don't know what I thought. It all seemed surreal."

"Ironically," Tania Tee says, "it was Julie's first husband who arrived on the scene, was it not?"

"That's right," Julie says. "We talked about it later, and he said he'd been wondering when something like this was going to happen."

(Crowd gasps)

"So," Billie G. says. "I gave my statement right there. Juanda's boyfriend and the guy I was dating at the time came and stayed with me. None of us slept that night. We just stayed up all night holding each other, crying."

"And what did you do the next day?" Tania Tee asks.

"Well," Billie G. says. "Every day for the next week we went into Charlottesville and took part in the protests."

"And who were you protesting against?" Tania Tee asks.

"Same thing everyone else was protesting against, I guess," Billie G. says. "White, heterosexual, protestant, conservative males."

"And why was that," Tania Tee asks?"

"Because they fit the profile. Homophobic, transgenderphobic, xeonophobic racist Nazis filled with hate, through and through, who go around murdering anyone who's not like *them*. Like Timothy Gardener. We viewed him as one from their ranks, so we went after them all."

"Billie G.," Tania Tee says. "Can you hold that thought? Can we come back to that?"

"Sure," Billie G. says.

"Mr. Dr. Byron Blevins," Tania Tee says, walking down to the end of the guest panel. "It's your turn to talk now."

(Crowd laughs)

"Was Timothy Gardener all those things Billie G. just said?" Tania Tee asks Blevins.

"No," Blevins says. "I mean, he was white and was assigned the male gender at birth, but that's where it ends."

"Can you tell us, Mr. Dr. Blevins, in your professional opinion as a psychiatrist, why did Timothy Gardener murder Juanda Cruz and then turn his gun on himself?"

"Look," Blevins said. "Timothy Gardener was so out of touch with reality by the time this thing happened, he wouldn't have known up from down, hot from cold, or wet from dry. He didn't kill that poor woman because he was a white, male, homophobe, whatever the papers called him, and whatever the protesters said about him. He killed that woman, because the man was a lunatic. If it hadn't been her, that night, it would have been someone else, on a different night, or on some other day. He was a timebomb waiting to go off, and it's just pure *irony* that his victim ended up being a transgender person of color with immigrant heritage."

"And why is this *ironic*?" Tania Tee asks.

"Because, and I know it's hard to believe, but those are the types of people that Timothy Gardener, back when he was *stable*, would have gone to bat to support *most*."

(Crowd gasps in disbelief)

"But once again," Blevins continues, "this whole tragedy allowed the media to jump in and name a devil- this concept of the Nazi white male in America- and name a victim, in this case a victim due to *mulitple* protected group status- gender identification, sexuality, race, ethnic background- and they were able to sell a lot of papers, get a lot of clicks on the internet, and make a whole lot of money by getting everyone to hate everyone else without anyone even *thinking* to stop and ask what was at the root of the problem. Let's just say it was because one group hated another, and then let's all the rest of us go hate that other group back! It's the media's oldest, most popular, and sadly, most effective play."

"You keep beating around the bush here, Mr. Dr. Blevins. "I'm tryin' to ask you, what was at the root of the problem?"

"The root of the problem," Blevins says, "is that Timothy Gardener was living a lie. He was a gay man, in the least, trying to live the life of a straight man. Frankly, I think the man was pansexual, like many people *truly* are, but I *did* know him to have homosexual tendencies."

"Can you explain what it means to be pansexual, Mr. Dr. Blevins?" Tania Tee asks. "I know my audience knows what it means, but we've probably got some online viewers who don't. And then, after that, fill us in on these homosexual tendencies you knew of Timothy Gardener to have."

"Sure," Blevins says. "'Pangender' basically means one is not defined by birth assigned gender, this concept of male or female, as far as how they see themselves and others in regard to gender or sexual preference. Pangender people can be attracted to men, women, transgenders, anyone, basically.

The can find themselves attracted to people who identify as straight, gay, bi, or whatever.

"The key with pangender people, as Billie G. stated earlier in regard to her friend Juanda, is that they can actually see the *person*, not the *package*. So they can be male, biologically, and fall in love with another biological male, and not actually be gay."

"Tania Tee already know all this," Tania Tee says. "But a lot of people can't grasp this concept. Why is this such a hard concept for most people, Mr. Dr. Blevins?"

"Because most people, frankly, are simply too closed minded," Blevins says.

(Crowd explodes- rises to their feet cheering)

"And these homosexual tendencies you talked about with Mr. Gardener?" Tania Tee says, motioning with her hands for the crowd to sit.

"Easy," Blevins said. "My husband and I had Julie and Timothy over for game night one night. Julie had been talking to me about leaving Timothy. This was after the whole porn thing with her son. Anyway, the whole time Timothy was at our house, he could *not* take his eyes off of my husband, and I even saw him rubbing his, well, you know, he was getting a freaking *boner* right there in the living room while staring at my husband. And it wasn't an issue of pangenderism, because he hadn't gotten to know anything about my husband and his personality, so it was simply about physical attraction- and hell, he *is* good looking and all, my husband- but this obviously made Timothy's attraction for him an issue of homosexuality, and not that there's anything wrong with that. Well, except for the fact that the man was married. To *me*!"

(Crowd giggles)

"The next day, when I talked to Julie about it," Blevins said, "I told her it was my professional opinion that she needed to get out of that relationship as quickly as she could. She confided in me that the only reason she'd stayed in the relationship so long was because she was already divorced once- it's called divorce guilt, and it's especially common when kids are in the picture- and she was *terrified* about the stigma of being divorced *twice*. She was certain no man would get near her again. She thought they'd all view it as if there was definitely something wrong with *her*, other than her obvious bad taste in men, at least with husband number two."

"Wrong!" Jeromy said.

(Crowd laughs)

"Look," Blevins continues. "It's this simple. Timothy Gardener refused to be who he was. He chose *not* to live the life that was meant for him to live. Now, I don't want to say it was because he was a coward, and because he didn't have the courage to come out of the closet like the rest of us have. His story is probably more common than most of us know. He probably had someone important to him in life, maybe a parent, or a close friend, who told him he'd better not be who he was. Think about, for example, the story of J. Egar Hoover and his mother. She knew who he was, and she always made sure to let her son know he'd better never let the rest of the world know who he was. And look at the lunatic *that* man became.

(Crowd moans 'uh-huh')

"It boils down to this," Blevins continues. "When we do not live the life that's meant for us to live. When we're scared to be who we are, despite what anyone else might think or say about it, we run the risk of becoming that which we hate, and we run the risk of hating, and in the case of Timothy Gardener, even killing, that which we love."

(Crowd moans a long, drawn out "ah" in understanding)

"That's pretty deep, Mr. Dr. Byron Blevins," Tania Tee says. "Billie G.," Tania Tee says, heading back up to the top of the panel. "Can we go back to what you were saying? Now, who were you protesting against after your friend was murdered?"

"Middle aged, white, heterosexual conservative males," Billie G. says, softly, with her head down.

"And why was that?"

"Because everyone was saying they were to blame, because they are homophobic, transgenderphobic, xeonophobic, racist Nazis."

"Was Timothy Gardener any of those things?" Tania Tee asks.

"Well," Billie G. says. "We thought…"

"Tania Tee ain't asking you what you *thought*, Billie G., Tania Tee asking you was Timothy Gardener any of those things?"

"No," Billie G. says.

"Peeps," Tania Tee says, turning to face the studio audience and the cameras recording for the livestream viewers at home. "We have *got* to stop fighting *hate* with *hate*. We have *got* to end the war we're having with each other right here in our own country. And we're the only ones who can *do* it. Us. Together. As one!"

(Crowd sits in silence- realizing Tania Tee is right- but not quite ready to applaud such insight)

"And that was the point of us being here today," Blevins says. "And it's not, by any means, to take up for people who hate others for being different or for any reason. Trust me, and I say this as a gay man, happily married to another gay man, both of whom do consider ourselves to be progressive liberals- and yes, we do vote democrat- we cannot continue to fight hate with hate. We cannot demonize people just because they don't think the way we do the same way they want to demonize us because we might not think like them. The only way for all of the hate in our society to stop is for us to stop the hate."

(Crowd explodes- everyone rises to their feet in applause- finally ready to cheer such insight)

"Let's move up to today," Tania Tee says. "Who wants to tell us what ya'll got going on to honor the memory of the late, beautiful Juanda Cruz?"

"I will," Mary Jane says. "We started a camp for LGBQT people."

"And everyone else, too," Adam adds. "It's inclusive for everyone. Anyone who might be feeling like a round peg trying to fit into a square hole at times is welcome. Struggles with sexuality or gender identification, though embraced by us, are not required. We want to let everyone know they are loved for who they are, no matter who that is.

"We were doing so well with our YouTube channel," Adam continues, "that we were able to buy a fifty acre tract of land that bordered the two acres we already had down in Scottsville. Sits right up against the James river. We originally were just planting trees in honor of the lost loved ones of our YouTube viewers on the property, but after we heard about what our old neighbor, that lunatic Timothy Gardener, did, we wanted to turn what we had going on into so much more, so we called Julie."

"Before my father died," Julie says, "he wrote grants for one of the biggest local not for profit groups in Charlottesville. You know," she says, pausing, "Come to think of it, Timothy used to go on and on about how my father owned the firm. I honestly thought he was joking. This was back when we first started dating. I thought it was his way of flirting with me, so I'd just laugh and go along, but… wow. I think he might have been serious."

"What's your maiden name?" Tania Tee asks.

"Schmitt," Julie says.

"What's the name of the firm where your father was a grant underwriter?" Tania Tee asks.

"The Schmidt Foundation," Julie says. "Schmidt with a 'dt' at the end. My maiden name was Schmitt with a 'double t' at the end."

Tania Tee raises her shoulders as if to say, 'well, you know,' and a half smile crosses her face, and light dawns across Julie's.

"Anyway," Julie continues, "Daddy was gone, but I still had contacts down there, and when I called my father's old firm, it turns out they were waiting on my call. As it turns out, the Overbaughs had already put up some money they wanted to go to a good cause, and they were hoping someone would come up with an idea that would allow us to honor Juanda, since she'd been renting from them and all that."

"Where the hell am I!" Mr. Overbaugh shouted, coming to.

"It's okay hon, we're on that real nice black lady's show. It's your turn to talk now."

"I can talk now?"

"Yes, Mr. Overbaugh." Tania Tee says. "We're talking about the money you put up for "Camp Color Me Loved."

"Is that what they're calling it?" Mr. Overbaugh says.

"Yes, dear," Mrs Overgaugh says. "We've been over this."

"Yeah," Mr. Overbagh says. "We sold that house that that Juanda woman lived in, despite it being where my wife's people lived for so long."

"This was a better cause," Mrs. Overbaugh said. "And we'll be gone soon. Whoever owns the property doesn't matter, because our family lineage ends with us."

"So we sold that property and a few others," Mr. Overbaugh continues, and we gave the money from the proceeds of the sales to the camp." With that, Mr. Overbaugh goes back to sleep.

"My father's old firm set up a 503-C," Julie says. "That's a not for profit organization- and we put the money donated by the Overbaughs into it, and we've already used some of the money to build several cabins and a pool, and we're inviting people to come out and camp, swim…"

"And fish right in the backyard, right there in the James River," Adam says.

"And we give free camel rides," Jeromy adds.

(Crowd laughs)

"And I've given my notice at the dealership," Billie G. says. "No more selling cars for me. I mean, I love my job, and I'll miss my demos…

(Crowd laughs)

"… but I loved my best friend more. I'm going to be general manager of the camp, and we're going to raise awareness, and we're going to do everything humanly possible to make sure that Juanda is remembered, and that people don't have to live a lie in silence and end up becoming a monstrous lunatic, like Timothy Gardener. We want to create a world where everyone is free to be who they are, no matter who that is, as long as it's not hurtful or hateful toward others.

(Crowd stands and goes wild)

"Before we move on to the second half of our show," Tania Tee says, facing the audience and the cameras, "I want to thank all of our guests here in the audience today, and I want to thank our viewers watching from home. I want to ask all of us to stop the hate. And let's not let *them*, whoever the hell the *them* are- be they the media or some political party- tell us who we're supposed to hate and why we're supposed to hate them. The good Lord created us all, and last time I checked, he didn't want us hating *anybody*."

(Crowd goes wild- gives standing ovation)

"Mr. Adam," Tania Tee says, turning now to face Adam. "I've gotta ask though, before we move on with our show, did you ever get back into writing?"

"Off and on," Adam says. "I'm actually thinking about writing a book about this situation. There are really *two* stories here, you see. The first, as Byron pointed out, is the story about the importance of being true to yourself. Being who you *are*, no matter who that *is*, or else, as Byron worded it, you risk becoming that which you hate and hating that which you love. And in this particular case, *killing* that which represents what you love."

"What's the other story?" Tania Tee asks.

"There is an entire story surrounding Timothy Gardener's outlook on life," Adam says. "A *hideous* outlook all caused by the fact that he lived a lie. The way he saw only a small part of a situation, or the way he might hear a small part of a story, and then the way he would completely fabricate the majority of the rest of the situation, or the story, in his sick mind, always making everyone *else* the bad guy. It's a story about the importance of not deciding to be judge, jury, and in this sad case, executioner, based upon knowing five per cent of someone's situation, and being completely oblivious to the other ninety five per cent, and then taking it upon yourself to make up the other ninety five per cent in your sick, hateful mind."

"That would be an interesting book," Tania Tee says. "Don't ya'll agree?" she asks, turning to the audience.

(Crowd applauds in agreement)

"What would you title a book like that, Mr. Adam?" Tania Tee asks.

"That's easy," Adam says. "The Lunatic."

The End

*If you enjoyed 'The Lunatic,' consider reading Kevin E Lake's other novels and short story collections which are available in print or Kindle format on Amazon. Also, consider watching Lake and his family on their YouTube channel, 'Homesteading

Off The Grid,' where, potentially, you may even see a Bigfoot Sasquatch...

...or a two humped camel named Sally!

***

**No camels were injured during the writing of this novel.

Made in the USA
Middletown, DE
25 June 2021